To all those who have held my heart...

To all those who have stomped on or shattered it...

To all those who have picked it up and caressed it
tenderly...

To all those who have rejected and redirected it...

To all those who have remained steadfast as I let my
misshappen heart reform and open again...

You have all taught me what love really is.

All of you.

Thank you.

Author note

This series was born from my own inquiry on love. Not only as a woman on the post-divorce dating journey, but as a friend, watching so many others stuck or struggling, and as a therapist, supporting both women and men navigating what has become an increasingly complicated journey. I have been looking at love through an epic kaleidoscope.

Some of the characters, scenarios and life lessons that appear within the pages of this series have been inspired by lived experiences (my own or others), while others have been born out of my desire to witness or experience something different to what we are being modelled. A way of loving that is more indicative of the world I wished we lived in… the world we can create by loving each other well.

Part of my writing process was to unpack my thoughts on all the reasons why love eludes us. To put my kaleidoscope into words. *Love Sex Poetry Peace* is a fiction series. However, I decided to take my initial creative process and turn it into an accompanying non-fiction multi-media series, drawing on my roots as a self-help author. This is my gift to you.

Heal for Love is a four-part series where you can delve into what it means to love and be loved in our mad modern world. At the beginning and end of each book you'll notice a QR code that invites you to bridge from the fictional fantasy world of *Love Sex Poetry Peace* into your own real-life inquiry on love. Choose your own adventure.

Whether you delve into your own inner work, or decide to immerse yourself solely in the protagonist, Lena's journey, I wish you a meaningful, heart-opening read.

Natalia Rachel

Heal for Love Multi-media Series

Heal for Love is a complimentary philosophy and self-help experience that has been designed to inspire a re-imagining of love and relationships and support you as you engage with your own healing work.

If you're ready to delve into the way you give and receive love to support greater connection, intimacy and reciprocity... this series is perfect for you!

Other Lovers

Volume #1
Love Sex Poetry Peace
The Series

Natalia Rachel

Listen, lover...

All I ever wanted was to be loved. I think it's all anyone of us really wants underneath it all. And for many of us, that unconscious hunger for love finds us chasing everything that love is not... a tragic lover's paradox.

I got married young. Nearly two decades later, I woke up one day and realized that what my marriage was built on was not love at all. And that who I'd become within it was so far from the best version of myself. So, I left. It was here, as a divorced mother of two, halfway across the world as an expat in tropical Singapore, that my journey to learn to love really began.

Before there could be love, I needed to take a hard look in the filter-less mirror. Not only at all my middle-aged jiggly bits (gosh, dating later in life is honestly the pits when it comes to body-image shit), but also study the she-monster ego self that was sitting brushing her blonde hair, batting her false eyelashes back at me in the mirror. I needed to meet the terrified little girl inside me who was still playing out her childhood trauma with the poor dudes who were wining and dining me. And I needed to examine the cold hard inner-bitch that kept pushing love away. She'd been trying to protect me, but she was keeping me stuck in a loveless limbo.

I also needed to get naked. A lot. To let the sensual goddess who had been a silent sleeping beauty inside me emerge. She needed to ride those man-rides without shame, and let generations of unshed tears fall to the earth... freeing herself, one romantic interlude at a time; one massive ugly cry at a time.

My other lovers became my teachers. Therapy became my temple. My girlfriends became my family. My body became an instrument of sensual bliss and honest wisdom. And my poetry became my sacred sense-making process.

The poems and stories I'm sharing with you now contain the lessons I have learned.

The traps.

The shadows.

The essential heartbreaks.

The illusions.

The fantasies.

The cold hard realities.

All of it.

As you read, you'll see it's in some ways non-linear, and in other ways, completely linear. Love does not have a timeline. Love does have a requirement for us to destroy all that love is not.

Love.

Sex.

Poetry.

Peace.

May there be plenty for us all.

Love,

Lena xx

Part 1 Loveless

Loveless

We found ourselves here

Loveless.

And while we

Blamed

Everyone else

And named

A thousand reasons

Why we were

Hurting here

In the end

It was all down to us.

Love is lost

In times of survival

Yet it is surely

The only thing

That will take us

To the other side.

The wicked world

We weave

Keeps luring us

Further away from

Love

And then trying to

Sell it back to us

In a thousand forms.

The real rebellion

Is to realize

That love

Will never be

A currency

No matter how

Hard

We try to flog it.

Love is not for sale.

Many Worlds

As I sit in the unknown

I feel all the timelines

Spreading themselves out

Before me

So many

That I could skip right into

Each one with

Incredible futures

Each one with losses

Some of them too heavy

To hold in my mind's eye.

Straddling all these

Worlds

Leaning in

Repelling back

Not sure which world

I belong in

Catching the fear rise

in my throat

And swell in my belly

Then letting it go again

Again

And again

And again

Remembering

The nest I have built

Inside my heart

And the net

Of the folks

Who cradle my cheek

And give me a swift

Tap on the butt

To propel me forward

Remembering

That I don't have to choose

Just one

That I am meant for

Many worlds

Weaving them as I walk

Towards the things

That bring me alive

The things

That bring me peace

And the people

The ones who remind me who I am.

Joseph was a sweetheart. But a troubled one. I met him at the tender age of 15 years old in the local Sydney Pizza shop where we both worked. Him driving salty laden pizzas to nearby homes, and me a sassy waitress with sparkly shoes and butterfly clips in my hair. It was *not* love at first sight. Not in the slightest. I found him awkward and strange with his dark mohawk, eyebrow ring and baggy pants. To be honest, I had my eyes on Harry, the pizza chef. His golden curly surfer hair and wide pearly smile had all the girls batting eyelashes and opening their young legs far too easily and often. But there was something inviting about Joseph's quiet adoring stare and his inquisitive questions, clearly besotted with the cute young thing that I was back then. I think I liked that he had his eyes on me.

For any of us neglected girls, being the object of attention or affection is the slipperiest turn on... and quite often a trauma bond waiting to happen.

While I never hooked up with Joseph during those playful pizza shop days, many years later, I ran into his open arms, on one of the darkest days of my youth. He was a daisy of a man. Sweet and unassuming, and I subconsciously knew that he would never, ever hurt me. At least not in the ways that I had been hurt by men before... and they'd been countless.

Joseph became my life raft in the wicked sea of life. And I unwittingly became his.

All it took was his kind presence, the stroke of my hair and a place to stay… and I was his.

Seventeen years later, through marriage, IVF, two children, one great whopping mortgage, a bunch of psychological breakdowns (his, not mine), detox centers and the onset of my mystery illness that seemed to be degenerative… I came to realize that perhaps this paradigm we had co-created needed to change. There was sickness here. Signs of systemic discord.

We had recently moved from Sydney, Australia to sunny Singapore, the land of ease and abundance, and something about the new-found support of this set-up led to a miraculous physical healing for me.

Long afternoons in the sunshine, laying by the pool. Floating, looking up at the palm trees and clear sky, letting my poor, tired body restore itself. Steamed rice, fish and Asian greens and ripe orange papaya, instead of endless pasta, bread and sugary things wrapped in plastic. Weekly acupuncture appointments and reflexology at the nearby Chinese clinic. The firm pressure of those old wrinkly Chinese men's hands, demanding that my feet stop clawing to the earth… to surrender to their ancient wisdom. Qi Gong in the Botanic Gardens with the other expat mothers who were also trying to adapt to a new world. Trailing spouses, seeking meaning. And my live-in maid, Coral, who played with my children while I slept, cried and healed. Ran me a bath. Told me, "It's ok, Ma'am. I will help you, Ma'am." She was perhaps the most unexpected and powerful gift of the whole experience. Someone to support me. More mother, less maid, to be honest.

Under the magic of the eastern sun, I began to reform. I could feel illness and fatigue exiting and the restoration of my primordial life force that had been lying dormant for so long.

Along with my growing vitality came the rising sound of my spirit that said... "There is something more for you, Lena. And if you stay in this marriage, you'll never know your true path. You'll never know your true love. You'll never know your true self. It's time to leave."

And so, I listened.

And my world became mad for a moment.

Divorce was such a dirty word back then. It wasn't yet 'in vogue'.

In some ways, my split came as a shock, but in other ways not at all. My life choice was well-received by no one. In fact, it did (and sometimes still does) come with spoonsful of judgement that I have learned not to let become my shame.

Joseph and I had been losing resonance in every area of life. The two places where we felt connected were in the 'business' of marriage and in the joy and duty of raising our precious children, Saskia and Cliff.

In all other areas, there was discord and disconnection.

He wanted heavy metal. I wanted pop.

He wanted burgers, I wanted sushi and salad.

He wanted whisky, and I wanted green tea.

He wanted to screw me any time he could.

I wanted to close my legs tight and tell him to go get it somewhere else and
LEAVE ME ALONE!

And one day, I did.

His love languages were gifts and acts of service.

I don't think I even knew what mine were back then. Love was full of obligations.

That December, we were on holiday in Langkawi, and he was making every effort to soften the energetic wrapping I'd placed around my pissed off pussy. Carrying the bags, flowers and a note waiting in the hotel room, taking the kids to swim so I could go have a massage. But these little living love notes were not unconditional. They came with the expectation of being a landing place for his lazy cock. Turning my body into a safe soothing cave for all his deep-seated self-worth shit and conditioned unconscious male entitlement.

Through that year, I'd become strong and sort of psychologically independent, spiritually aware. And with this newfound embodiment, I finally set one clear unshakable boundary.

"My body is closed to you, Joseph," I stated as I looked him squarely in his confused brown puppy-dog eyes. "Forever," I added, so that there was no confusion.

In that moment, I broke his heart.

But I also finally set my body free from years of being 'in service' of his needs and total abandonment of my own.

His middle-aged body filled and puckered with every emotion under the sun. Grief, confusion, anger, fear, shame. All of it.

Anger was a new one for him.

And about a week later, when I finally extended the message to let him know I wanted out of the marriage, that anger rose up like a fucking dragon that had been sleeping inside him for forty-something years.

The fire and ash of his rage engulfed me for a few days. And I knew intuitively that this rising and release was for his highest good, and mine too.

So, I sat very still as his psychological volcano erupted. It took a lot of self-regulation and self-trust. To be honest, part of me was terrified, but this piece of me had been activated, my higher self perhaps, and I knew that this was a moment of co-creative transformation.

After the fire settled, we sat together in the rubble of it, the air of our marriage thick with disappointment, trembling together. Here, our journey to conscious co-parenting began. We had no map for it. So, we drew one. Together.

He agreed that he had not been happy for years yet had not been brave enough to speak it. He was ready to find a new way where we could be supportive co-parents.

Our co-parenting journey has gone through many iterations, from finding 50/50 status quo, to welcoming new partners and stepchildren into the fold, to me exploring a semi-nomadic international lifestyle and finally finding a new international co-parenting dynamic. It was never about money and assets. In fact, I made sure that we focused our efforts on peace, harmony and freedom first. I didn't walk away from my marriage with alimony or property. I walked away from a partnership that was life draining (for both of us) and transitioned into one that continues to be life-giving. The proof is in the clearly secure, wise and playful little souls of our children, Saskia and Cliff. The security of Joseph's new blended family. And the freedom and peace from which I breathe and move each day. An extraordinary life.

I see all the future timelines of my life laid out before me regularly. The paths I could walk. The women I could become. And I know that no matter which one I choose to walk, Joseph will be there, loving our children and quietly supporting me as my conscious co-parent.

Instead of marriage, there is simply support.

And if I think back to the day that our romance bloomed amidst our young pain, that's exactly what I was looking for.

Bad Bitch, Good Girl

There's a part of me

That's a dirty bitch

But she's been

Condemned

To a foreign prison

By my good girl prude.

In moments

I feel her

Climbing the bars

And jangling

Her slut chains.

Flutters in my core

Pangs in my pants

Then I tell her

"Bad girl

Shut up

You're not welcome here."

I purse my lips

And flash

My pearly whites

Bored to tears

By the suited sods

Across the dinner table.

Uninspired

By my thousandth

Self-administered orgasm.

Occasionally

I let her out of prison

For a short parole

But she's shellshocked.

Freedom has become

Too foreign

And this world

Ruled by messed up men

Has no idea

How to receive her.

She'll end up

Tied up somewhere

Or shattered

In a gutter

So I keep sending her

Back to prison

It's safer there.

But her ache

Is my ache

Her rage

Is my rage

Her longing

Is my longing.

And as I begin

To meet her

In the mirrored hallway

Of my inner world

The chains and bars

Vanish.

No more separation

Between slut and prude

Bad bitch or good girl

Just one woman

Unabashed

Owning it all.

And so, I entered the jarring jungle of middle-aged dating. Like a fawn finding my feet, I had to learn how to dress, dance, swipe, sit, undress and receive foreign fingers and cocks who were roaming in search of a slut or a slave.

After seventeen years in the straitjacket of marriage, and a year of finding my feet as a single mama, I ripped off the band-aid and began the search for romance, sex and something more.

To be naked with all my wobbly bits and furry fanny felt deliciously terrifying. At first, I had to have the lights dimmed and my eyes closed, braced with the fear of judgement and rejection. But I soon learned that most men in this quirky dating pool of leftovers and misfits were simply happy to feel a body open to them. A fold of fascia was a tasty love handle and the dimples on my thighs were either inconsequential or invitations to lick, kiss or bite a bit.

But I wasn't used to dating without the intention to mate and bind. My conditioning told me that romance and sex should lead to marriage, or some kind of structural commitment. So, I found myself in a loop of desire, shame and confusion.

There was clearly some kind of 'bad bitch' inside me who wanted to play, fuck, squirt and dance into the sunset. She'd been unleashed the moment some nameless man buried his head between my legs in a hotel room on Orchard Road. My ex-husband had never pleasured me that way. I don't think I would have let him. I'd been locked inside my poor abused body for so long and our sex life had been about me acquiescing to his incessant demands for gratification. It had never been about my enjoyment.

Laying on a standard queen bed with over-starched sheets, staring at the anonymous beige curtains in that mid-range hotel room, this dude's tongue woke the sexy serpent inside me. He, himself, was a faceless blip in the saga of my life, but the hunger he ignited remained. Once my sex-tap turned on, I found myself wanting to get naked with any decent-looking chap who'd buy me dinner. The 'bad bitch' was alive.

But my 'bad bitch' didn't exist inside me alone. She was co-living with the 'good girl' inside me who was far more familiar. A prude who tied sexuality with commitment. In fact, to her, sexuality didn't really exist. Sex was full of obligations, expectations, warped authority and silent shame. So, she and the sensual slut that was emerging were at complete odds.

After my 'bad bitch' would lay down and grace the air with her orgasms, my 'good girl' would want to cuddle, grip on like a baby koala bear, plan the next date and fantasize about a future with whatever poor stranger had leant me his body that evening. This inner conflict triggered all kinds of weird dynamics. Either the men would run a mile (clinger alert!), or they would try and lock me down so tightly, I'd be the one racing for hills. Bad behavior all round. Ghosting, dumping, breadcrumbing, disappearing, reappearing, tears, frustration... why was this so damn hard? It wasn't only the men playing games with me. I was just as bad, either batting them around in some feline game or slamming the gates shut at the first sign of contradiction or potential heartache.

"You shouldn't sleep with them so soon," finger-wagged Ellen, my wise bestie who was determined to coach me into a version of myself who could hook my next husband.

Ellen was a native New-Yorker, in her mid-fifties, on her second marriage and living a total next level life. She'd come into my world at a time when I was crumbling under the weight of divorce and financial ruin. She held my broken heart and desolate soul with the sweetest care but also a kind of grit that demanded that I do better. "Put your big girl pants on and adjust that crown on your head," she'd remind me in my lowest moments.

Ellen was the epitome of an empowered woman. She had the man, the wealth, the jet-setter dream and was flawless to a fault. When she walked into a room in her designer dresses, she commanded attention even though she was only five foot two and didn't flaunt her flesh. But she did have certain ideas of how to 'catch the guy', which I sometimes listened to, and other times rebelled against. She was like the living reflection of my inner 'good girl'. The angel on my shoulder.

"Just fuck 'em all. There's no shame in that," chanted Charlie. If Ellen was the reflection of my inner 'good girl' and the angel on my shoulder, Charlie was the reflection of my inner 'bad bitch' and the devil on the other.

Charlie was in her late forties, childless by choice, a rebel and adventurer who embodied the liberated feminine. Though she was German born, she'd lived all over the world since she was little, having come from a family of diplomats. She was a beautiful queen bee, buzzing from flower to flower. Fucking who she wanted, when she wanted, earning like a boss and flowing with the winds of the world. Nothing nor no one could trap or diminish her.

These two beautiful brave women were equalizers as I navigated this new post-divorce world. While Ellen was planning her next international rendezvous with her husband, who was awaiting her command, Charlie was exploring the matrix of secret sex parties and planning what her future polycule would look like. And I was torn, craving a little bit of both their realities, trying to conjure up my own. The inner conflict often caused me to feel like an anxious, hot mess failure of a woman.

Society said I should catch my next beau.

Rebellion said I should fuck to my heart's content and cut those dumb dudes loose.

While I wanted to lean into rebellion, society had my psyche tied up, and I couldn't seem to enjoy casual sex. It always left me feeling full of shame, despair and desolation.

Was I just not built for casual relationships?

Was I built only to mate?

Or did I need to work thought some kind of patriarchal/matriarchal bull-fuckery in order to shag with abandon?

Enter Leonardo.

I decided to make a concerted effort to find my sexual liberation, so I set out to swiping on Tinder. Quite quickly, I matched with Leonardo, a six-foot-five, half-Italian half-Czech scientist hunk of a man. I didn't know much else other than he was tall, ripped and European. He'd do for this, just nicely.

The conversation on the day we met at the beach bar wafted in one ear and out the other. I wasn't here to bond; I was here to get rammed. After some eyelash batting over drinks, we went for a walk on the pier and as I coyly looked up at him, he placed his confident large hand behind my neck and pulled me close and pressed his lips against mine. Fireworks like I had never felt before tickled my skin, and I was instantly ready for him.

Back at my condo, he discarded my new midnight blue Victoria's Secret corset and panties like a pro, and proceeded to tease, tantalize and delight me in ways I had never even had the guts to imagine. I felt safer and more open than I had ever felt with a man before. Maybe I could do this casual sex thing after all.

Afterwards, as I was laying in his arms, he asked, "Can I sleep here? I want to be close with you." I was momentarily confused, as every other man up till this point could not wait to extricate himself from my bed after he'd shed his semen.

My voice quivered. "Sure, Leonardo." I was sleepy and submerged in the post-orgasm oxytocin ocean, and the idea of staying in it with him a little longer felt enticing. I snuggled into his big, toned body, laying my head over the wolf tattoo on his chest... and slept like a love-drunk baby.

It was never meant to be more than sex. But something happens when you lay night after night in a pool of orgasms and oxytocin. Bonding is inevitable.

And for those of us who hold unresolved trauma, the moment we bond, the moment the trauma presents for healing.

About ten sultry sessions into our sexcapades, we were getting a bit more abandoned, and his wild wolf began to emerge. Mid-fuck, he took his proud paw and slapped my right butt cheek. Not too hard, but hard enough to trigger me into a state of trauma. It was as if I was ten years old and my father's hand was beating my frightened body.

As the flashbacks came, my body froze. I'd done enough healing work on this particular trauma narrative and felt safe enough with Leonardo to quietly say, "Stop... I'm having an abuse flashback."

Immediately, Leonardo's demeanor shifted, and he scooped me into his caring arms and stroked my hair. "You're safe, my mermaid. You're safe, you're safe," he crooned. I loved his pet name for me; it made me feel instantly seen, and a little bit safer. I wept in his arms, and he kept stroking my hair and kissing me gently on my forehead. He patiently waited for me to stop shaking and whimpering and said, "Tell me."

I shared a little about my childhood abuse and this memory of being beaten on my right buttocks by my father while laying frozen in the shower.

"I will never ever hurt you. You must know that," he affirmed with his thick eastern European accent. "I won't slap your butt again."

I giggled and sniffed at the same time. "You can slap my left butt... softly," I replied. And we lay in arms sharing stories from our childhood, kissing tenderly and learning about each other's fractured hearts till we fell asleep in the early hours.

After that, I knew it wouldn't be possible to be casual with Leonardo. My heart had opened and oriented to him. The thing was, he wasn't available for more. Not really.

He'd mentioned early on that he was separated. But what I learned through snippets of post-coital conversation was that he was amid a messy battle with his wife and had a special needs child back in Europe. His heart was not so sure he could leave the family.

While I yearned for there to be more between us, I told him that we couldn't continue because it was a recipe for drama and broken hearts. I told him to fly back to Italy where his wife and son were waiting at their summer home in Tuscany. And that, if he should ever find himself truly free, to look me up.

I cried for days and days and days. Ellen took me for a pedicure and a long lunch to cheer me up. "He's not your future husband," she said. "He's only a chapter in your story and you deserve a man who is free and clear and ready to love you well. Your perfect man is on the way. You're right on track."

After a few weeks of grieving, I was able to make peace with and find gratitude for the experience. I was pretty sure I had healed my fear of the masculine. Leonardo was unlike any man I had ever been with. Big, brash, bold and charismatic. I had always chosen meeker men, who could never hurt a fly. A symptom of the past abuse I endured. I was always in control, wearing the pants and sure of my position of power.

Something shifted post-Leonardo. Some kind of sexual awakening where my 'bad bitch' didn't feel so bad anymore. And my 'good girl' didn't clamp down my cooch so tight. There was a new kind of freedom growing inside me. A psycho-sexual integration that broke me free from the polarities of society vs. rebellion, safety vs. fear, or validation vs. shame. I was just one wild woman, with nothing to fear, nor hide.

Point Of Origin

There is no war in my body.

There is no war in my home.

There is no war in my words.

There is no war in the way I walk through the world.

May this be true for us all.

After several triggering dating experiences, I decided to take a pause and look inwards. My healing needed to take top priority. I'd been talking about my various romantic encounters with my long-time therapist, Tabitha. I'd been a practicing therapist myself for many years, and part of my commitment to service was to engage in my own therapy work. Therapy for the therapist.

Each week, I'd sit in her cozy treatment room on the faded brown velvet couch, feet up and snuggled under a crochet blanket with a cup of licorice tea. She'd peer at me though her purple spectacles with her crinkly eyes full of compassion and wisdom, as I would often vomit out a story about some new man that had surprised, shocked or seduced me. Her crazy curly grey hair joined in the conversation as she shook or nodded her head to validate whatever rant I was on.

Sometimes there'd be three new men to name in a week, whereas other times, it would be a few weeks unpacking my feelings about one poor sod who'd become part of my attachment theory processing.

My disorganized attachment became a heightened daily experience. Anxiety and abandonment issues rising every time I was waiting for a text message, eyes glued to my phone, heart beating loudly in the cage of my chest, and making up scenarios of being dumped or ghosted. I'd crave daily communication, check-ins, care, chats from men I had only just met. And when I didn't get it, I'd turn them into an asshole or tell myself "He's just not that into you." Of course, sometimes that would be the case, but more often than not, they were simply living their lives and not in the treacherous vortex of trauma-dating. Ironically, when certain men did show up communicating clearly and consistently, I would feel suffocated and find myself not wanting to reply for days or turn them into some loser in my mind. Projections and stories. Stories and projections.

In hindsight, I now know it is very normal for our unresolved childhood trauma to rear itself up in the journey to love. And that our fast-paced paradigm of clicks, texts, emojis and reading between the lines makes it far worse than it really needs to be.

But at this point, I was like a stressed-out toddler and the superhighway of love was feeling fast, furious, unkind, and confusing. And I was leaking far too much energy on it. I'd regularly be too anxious to get my work done or crying in the bathtub, feeling abandoned and not good enough. "Why am I like this?" I would ask myself regularly. "What's wrong with me?"

Most of what I was experiencing was not about these men. It was all inside me. The conflict, the distress, the grief, the rage, the pain, the ocean of longing. While I'd already been in therapy for some time, I decided to take healing my heart more seriously. To end the internal war that seemed to spark with every man I met and redraw the lay lines of my heart that had been so clearly maligned and malformed. To stop projecting my trauma into the world like some never-ending war of hearts.

The moment I took my sweet aching heart into my compassionate care, the dating game changed. It became a journey of listening and learning, rather than a string of wins or losses. My agenda became to know my own heart. And with this, there were no more perpetrators or kings in my story. The war of hearts was over (at least for a while).

Precious Metal

Plastic People

Wandering the world

Tight & Taught

Roped into

The matrix

Smiling without souls

Signals

Of dissociation

Skeletons & wigs

And designer trinkets.

I can see their

Spirits

Floating above their

Heads

Aching to descend

Into barren bodies

That just can't

Welcome them.

Or trapped

Chained up inside

Some dark corner

Of their ribcage

Underneath

Unconscious armor

Walking

Aimlessly

In this magnetic

Labyrinth

Of pixels and putrid

Junk.

No wonder

My heart

Feels lonely

Here.

As it beats

In my body

Looking for others

Who are sitting

Inside themselves

Rather than

Lost in some

Other dimension.

The forgotten

Jungle

Of folks

Is getting

Crowded.

Yearning

Yearning

Yearning

To say hello

With my cells

And have my

Humanity

Echoed through

Energy.

Wading

Through plastic

Looking for

Pure

Precious

Metal.

Programming

My heart

To keep

Orienting

Detecting

Travelling

Even though

It grows weary.

I know you're out there.

The more curious I got about my own 'map for love', the more clearly I could see others'. It was as if I could see the dotted lines of their heart compass and all the stale stitches with the dried blood of wounds past that required cleaning, opening; some kind of psychic surgery.

Most of the men I'd meet were totally disconnected from the painful stories that were sitting inside their chests or the way they projected them onto the world. They were either unconscious terrors or shutdown shells. And I simply couldn't find a way to connect.

Once the lightbulb of heart consciousness had switched on inside me, I began to feel lonelier than ever. I wanted to connect from a place of awareness, compassion, insight and inquiry. Yet as I swiped, and drank, and dined and walked with these guys, it was so rarely possible. I felt like I was walking in a different dimension. I'd flick between putting myself on some kind of spiritual pedestal or lopping back to self-pathology and shame. Total polarity. Either there's something wrong with them, or there's something wrong with me.

"Love is a miracle," chimed Ellen after one of my semi-regular depressive downloads. "It's so rare for two people to fall in love that when you find someone you actually want to spend time with, it's a blessing. Stop looking for love and look for little blessings."

I rolled my eyes.

It's easy for you to say with your fancy husband and glamorous life, I thought but didn't dare say. What emerged from my pouting mouth was "Ok, ok. I'll be patient."

Patience was not a virtue I had yet learned, in any respect.

I couldn't help but feel hopeless on the dating front. It felt like my options were getting worse over time. I honestly think Covid did some dramatic damage to the dating pool. To humans in general. We'd all learned to be alone, stay inward, connect online, drugged up with social media and a million zoom meetings. Dissociated, disconnected drones. It was easier to connect with someone's avatar than their actual human form. So even when I'd get excited about meeting a potential match online, I'd turn up and find that they were nothing like their profile or the pretty projection I'd painted in my mind. Sometimes the conversation was so stale, I had to stifle a yawn. On occasion, I'd find myself mid-yawn in the middle of date. A sure sign we were on the road to nowhere. And every time I'd leave, I'd feel disappointed and alone.

Sitting with this loneliness took me to the land of grief. Big swollen tears would escape my eyes on the evenings I was sitting in my little Singapore home. It was worse on nights when my children were at their dad's place. I'd count down the days till they would come back and smother them in kisses, excited to hear about their past few days. On the bright side, sitting with such epic loneliness made me such a grateful mama, always excited to engage. I'd think about some of my traditionally married mama friends who were trying to both parent fulltime and work and how cranky they got with their kids, always awaiting the next escape for grown up time. And I'd also think of some of the single female therapy clients I had, who endured their loneliness day in day out. Polarity again. And I tried to meet my situation with gratitude and welcome the grief of loneliness that was a regular visitor throughout a good few years.

Aside from honoring and accepting my grief, I also set a boundary with it.

I was not going to wallow when there was connection ready and waiting with the wonderful women in my life. I decided to curate dinner parties with my favorite women. One sunny September evening, I invited a great group of girls for a Thai-style feast chez moi.

Ellen and Charlie were there in a heartbeat. Because they were such polar opposites, there was always a bit of a sizzle in the air when they got in the same room. Some eye rolling, some snippy comments, some huffing and puffing, but all in good jest and with a dose of laughter and play. Oh, how I loved these two vastly different creatures. Ellen arrived in her Dolce dress and Valentino shoes, while Charlie rocked up in her string bikini, barely over the bum denim skirt and dusty hiking boots.

Then there was darling Esther. I'd met Esther at an art gallery opening in New York a few months back and our friendship was newly blossoming. Esther was a gift that kept on giving. As I began to know her, it was as if I was continuing to unwrap layers of love, wisdom and generosity. I regularly felt pangs in my heart, so grateful to know such a humble, talented, giving and powerful woman. Esther was a Chinese-Australian ex-concert violinist who had made her way up in the international arts scene and flew around the world to produce multi-disciplinary events. She was based in Sydney, my hometown, but regularly in Singapore working with the Tourism Board on high profile projects. In the group setting, she was more of a listener than a leader, but when her make-up free mouth opened, her words always sliced through whatever conversation we were having. I think everyone (including me) tended to underestimate Esther. She was a quiet watchful presence with her silvery hair and simple style that never shouted. Over time, I came to believe she was perhaps the most powerful and unconditioned or unfiltered of us all.

The last one to make up our quintet was Naomi. Naomi entered my life when I was in the transition from illness to wellness. We'd locked eyes in an airport lounge in Singapore. She was in transit from India where she'd been visiting her family, and I was on the way to Sydney for a medical treatment. In fact, it was my last medical treatment before I decided to say goodbye to doctors and dosages and hello to the world of natural medicine and somatic trauma processing. I truly believe there was some divine intention that brought us together on that day. After an hour of chatting at the airport, Naomi managed to wrangle us two upgraded business class seats together for the flight to Sydney.

Naomi was the kind of woman who could turn sand into silk. Her sparkling energy, paired with her luscious black locks and flawless face of a goddess, had people entranced. She was amidst her own transition, having decided to exit the distress of dating for an arranged Indian marriage, break her family and cultural norms, and do it her own way. Her decision had caused a certain amount of upset with her family, and she'd just flown back to try and make peace with her mother. The trip hadn't gone according to plan. And when we met, her face was stained with teary mascara streaks. It seemed as if we were both in incredibly transformational moments in our spiritual journeys, and there was some kind of reflection, recognition and affirmation we offered each other. On that trip to Sydney, I had been wearing three crystal bead bracelets. Listening to her stories, I decided to offer her the white speckled howlite one as a gift and reminder of our connection. She received it, gushing gratefully, and it stayed on her wrist for some years after.

In the group, she was somewhat of an equalizer. She was such a chameleon of a woman that she could either elevate or ground the energy, depending on what was truly needed in the moment. She was definitely a healer, even if she didn't fully know it yet.

As I sat with these incredible women who hailed from all over the globe, poolside in the tropical balmy Singapore evening, with a feast of papaya salad, prosecco and steamed basil and ginger seabass, I realized I was not lonely at all. The heart connection that I'd been seeking on my dates was right here... in the company of women. And it was these friendships that began to nourish my heart back to vitality and hopefulness.

Algorithm

Scanning

The grid

Around me

For signs

Of life

A kind

Available cock.

A human

Hungry

Fembot

Seeking to end

Her famine.

And the more she

Scanned

The more she

Starved.

Watching those

Other women

Swooping in

To claim their

Prey.

Doing their

Dick-led rain dance

Satiated

By thoughtless seamen

Yet lonelier

Than ever.

And as I sat here

Still yet scanning

Altered by the

Algorithm

And the disembodied

Sea of humanity

I decided to

Switch it off.

To stop seeking

And skip

Down to the ocean

Sunshine and seashells

My desperation disappeared

Into the waves

Off the grid.

Naomi and I were sitting in the window of a cute wine-bar in Soho, London, where we had made our global schedules meet. She was working on a charity gala funded by her not-for-profit and I was passing through to visit my aunt after teaching a training program in the Netherlands.

My pinot noir was purple and velvety, and the beef carpaccio and cheese plate accompanied one of my regular rants about dating disappointment.

"And what do you have to offer a guy?" questioned Naomi.

I was stumped by the question. Embarrassingly stumped. Of course, I had a lot to offer. But I'd been focusing so much on what I wanted to manifest in my man that I hadn't paused to consider what I wanted to give. My cheeks went pink. My glossed-up lips stayed still and slightly parted as I paused to find my words.

Naomi just got it. At forty, she was newly engaged after five years on the dating circuit, post fourteen years of being shopped around for a potential arranged Indian marriage. After meeting with matchmakers in India, New York and London with no 'success', she'd moved to Sydney and entered the dirty mainstream dating pool. She'd been through the rabbit warren of dudes, discards, betrayal, half-truths, sliding doors and many micro-heartbreaks. So, when she sat and listened, it was with a certain kind of empathy that my long-time married friends just couldn't quite muster. And when she called me out with her special kind of candor, it cut right through my poor damsel bullshit and snapped me back to look at my part in whatever story I was playing out.

"I don't know what I have to offer," I finally blurted and broke into an out-of-character public display of emotion. I'm an emotional creature. And crying is part of my regular repertoire, but it was usually done in the privacy of my home, hotel, in a restaurant toilet stall or the safety of a good friend's kitchen over a simple salad. And on planes. I did have a tendency to weep on planes without a care for what the poor passengers next to me might think.

Naomi placed a kind hand on my back and tsk-tsk-tsked. "You have so much to offer, babe. You're one of the most loving, wise and powerful creatures I have ever met. I only asked because it's important to think reciprocally... and get intentional with how you want to show up. You've become so focused on what kind of man you want to get that you're forgetting that it's a two-way street. Maybe it's blocking you?"

"You're fucking right," I replied. "I need to sit with that."

The rest of the evening was spent sharing details about our travels, work goals and getting excited about Naomi's wedding planning. She and her Aussie fiancé James were set to tie the knot in eighteen months at sunset in Uluru in the Northern Territory of Australia. It was going to be a sacred occasion in many ways.

Our conversation played on repeat in the outskirts of my mind for the rest of my trip, but it wasn't until I was back in Singapore, walking by the beach alone, that I really had time to pull it apart and process.

I realized that my dating life, for the last few years, had largely been experienced via apps. And I was sure that the swipe, delete, repeat culture of it was altering the way my brain processed men altogether.

Apps are like a series of fast-moving personal classifieds. We look at each 'commercial' for anywhere between a millisecond and three seconds and our brains quickly assess if this image and few accompanying words are a potential mate. We discard tens or perhaps hundreds of humans per swiping session (depending on how addicted or desperate we are). And when we do finally find a hallelujah of a match, we proceed to text-interview each other, as if we are applying for the great privilege of a date.

To be honest (and I am mortified to admit this), I had got all my first dates down to one-hour for drinks at the same bar within a walk of my apartment. I was so altered by the algorithm that I was trying to make dating as productive as possible. Minimal effort. They come to me. And I'd review their potential. They'd need to check off a bunch of things on my 'shopping list', make good conversation, and give me at least minimal butterflies... and if they didn't.... Next! Sometimes, I'd literally hop off my bar stool after leaving a date that was a 'hard no' and open whatever app I was using that week as I sashayed off down the street.

Next, next, fucking next.

As I reflected on this, I realized how awful it all was. And if I was behaving with such disgrace, then men were doing it, too. We were co-creating a digital hellhole of discarded hearts.

I didn't want to date like this.

I didn't want to turn men into a checklist, a product, or an object.

Even worse, when I thought about it, I realized that this algorithm-based way of searching for men had transcended the digital landscape and into the way I scanned a real-life room for potentials. My altered brain was creating a meat-market that was eternally understocked.

While I will always be first to admit I am far from perfect and can be as flawed and fucked up as the next person, I will also say that I am always quick to course-correct the moment I realize my part in any kind of dynamic funk.

So then and there, I deleted the two dating apps on my phone. It was time to exit the atrocious land of algorithms and see if I could heal my neural pathways back to some kind of graceful way of processing.

I had some kind of withdrawal for about two weeks. Evidence that those apps were a digital drug with clear psychological and social symptoms. The withdrawal showed up in phases. First, I'd keep reaching for my phone for some swiping time. And each time, I'd pivot to scrolling social media. I'd never been much into social media. I'd engaged with it very purposely and with a lot of healthy boundaries for work, but personally, it was never my dissociative tool of choice. I found that Instagram bored me to tears, and LinkedIn triggered my high-performance hustle Type-A part that I had really been working on softening. But I needed something to get through that first stage of withdrawal. My phone became my frenemy for a while.

The next stage was processing my sexual frustration. Luckily, I had a drawer of trusty vibrators to help me. In those two weeks of digital dating detox, I gave those toys the best run for their money. At least twice a day. Sometimes three. Often two or three orgasms per session. And after each orgasm, I'd either cry or scream and punch my pillow. I was letting out grief and rage through my yoni. I didn't want to sleep with any old (or young) idiot, but I did want to be having far more sex than I was having. Which, at that time, was a whopping zero.

Since my brief time with Leonardo, I'd become insatiable. He'd woken my inner sensual goddess, and she was hungry.... Starving.

After about two weeks, the itch to get back on the apps disappeared. I also noticed that I had stopped walking into rooms with eyes roaming. I'd righted my processing pathways, it seemed. And the low-level anxiety that had accompanied my app-appetite had disappeared. I was more grounded and peaceful. It helped that I was back to a pretty powerful self-care routine, with morning meditation, Qi Gong and a 'patience walk' at the beach five days a week.

I went to the same self-care spot every day. My spot was about fifty meters away from a group of older local Chinese practitioners and the whole area of the beach had a special vibe about it from our combined daily energy work. After practice, I'd often get a coffee and sit and write. Sometimes poetry, sometimes planning for a project, training content or notes for a team meeting. I felt like the most grounded and purest version of myself right after practice. In that spot, so many intentions, ideas and ventures were seeded.

One morning mid-practice, I noticed a tall, blonde, clean-cut man lay down his sports bag, kick off his shoes, remove his tank top, and run down into the ocean for a swim. I followed his athletic body out of the corner of my eye for a moment but stayed in my practice. I was doing an energy clearing and vitality building sequence to restore my energy after a three-day training program I had just finished teaching. But I could feel my mind following my eyes, wondering about this mystery man. There was rarely anyone new at my little spot, so I did myself a favor by shutting my eyes to refocus.

When I opened my eyes, I could feel his gaze before I turned my head to meet it. It was like a cool calming breeze. He was sitting shirtless only a few meters away, diamond drops of the ocean sparking on his fair, hairless skin. His blue eyes crinkled at the corners, and his lips made a slightly crooked close-lipped smile like a crescent moon reaching up to his left cheek. I think I was so in the moment that I didn't smile back, I just stared. I realized how weird I was being when he started chuckling, and I automatically averted my gaze, half annoyed with him, half annoyed with myself.

I wasn't used to organic meets. It never happened in Singapore. And why, oh why, did I have to be wearing the most unsexy yoga set today of all days? I had some pretty hot two-piece sets, but today I was wearing some old floral yoga pants that were a bit too big for me (so they didn't suck in my belly the way I'd like) and a boring black crop top that did no favors for my breasts, which could look quite fabulous in the right garment. I was make-up free with unbrushed bed hair and honestly not looking my best.

"What's that you were doing?" he asked with a slightly staccato Americanized Scandinavian accent.

"Qi Gong," I answered. His non-responsive face suggested he had no idea what I was talking about. "Like Thai Chi," I offered.

"Ah, I see," he replied. Then he looked away, silent for a while.

Okaaaaaaay, I thought, a little irked to be pulled out of my practice. I shook my head and opened my notebook to do some journalling... or maybe to distract myself from the encounter.

"How about you tell me all about it over coffee? Let me give you my number. No pressure." His invitation came with a much wider smile, the moon of his mouth reaching to both his cheeks this time. He stood up, walked over and handed me a piece of paper with his number. He gently placed a hand on my shoulder and said, "I'm Dylan, by the way. I hope you reach out. Have a pleasant day." And before I could let him know my name, he strode off.

I had a mixed response to the encounter. He was kind of sweet, but kind of nonchalant. I wasn't sure what to think of this fellow. He hadn't asked for my name or anything about me—a bit weird really—but then I looked down at the piece of paper in my hands and realized what had happened. A meet-cute! A real life, non-app, non-algorithm, non-me scanning the room, organic meeting. I was delighted and did a little sit-jig, pleased with myself. This was clearly the fruits of me deleting the apps and realigning my processing pathways... or a coincidence. Either way, I was pleased with myself.

I sat cross-legged on the grass, smiling out over the water, eager to share the moment. I fossicked my phone from my bag and called Charlie.

"Hey giiiirrrrl!" Charlie crowed as she answered the phone. "How are you?"

"You'll never guess what happened. I just had an old school meet-cute."

"Yay, yay, yay!" she celebrated. "Are you home tonight? Spicy margs and you can tell me all about it? I'm just heading into a boring traders conference. Yawn. Six pm?"

"You're on," I confirmed. "I'll pick up some limes."

Charlie had the most contradictory life. Trader by day, international DJ by night. Meet-cutes were par for the course for her. She was always telling me they were the best way to meet men. And meet men she did. She could ride with the old school corporate boys and party with the A-list party circuit or walk into a grocery store and take the bread out of some unassuming dude's basket in an attempt to start a flirty conversation, which usually worked for her. But these moments always seemed to elude me. She was part mogul, part magic, part mayhem. And I loved every bit of her. She was like a living invitation to play. Spicy Margs, music and girl time had become a ritual any time we were both in town. I smiled at the thought of our evening ahead.

I lay back on the grass and let the sun congratulate my freckly face.

This meet-cute felt like a sign. Like hope for an app-free love life. And although I knew it was only a number, and I knew nothing about him, I let myself lay there for a while, making up fantasies about this Dylan man. I had no profile, no checklist, no interview date planned. Just me and my trusty imagination... and his phone number. Maybe this was how it was meant to work. Maybe, just maybe, he could be the one. A girl can only dream.

Permission To Wait

I used to knock

On the door

Try and climb

Through an unlocked

Window

Finding those crevices

That were ajar

The slivers of air

Where I could compress myself

Just enough

To breathe in

And inch through

So quietly

That no one would notice.

And then one day

I realized

All that knocking

Turned me into

A wandering salesman.

And all that silent

Shapeshifting

Turned me into

A heavy

Trojan horse

Half animal

Half woman

Carrying so much

That was not mine

To bare.

All I was getting

Inside those castles

Was the thrill of arrival

The arms of authority

Who I had wanted

So dearly

To hold me close

But always ended up

Clenched around

My throat

In one way

Or another.

I'd find myself

Gasping

For air

Wanting to rip

The invisible chains

Off my body

And then shaming myself

For sensing

Their cold hard metal

At all.

My victories

Became villains

Inside me

And the world

I had been reaching for

That I had arrived at

Revealed itself

Not really

What I wanted

At all.

Validation means nothing

When it comes

With the vacation

Of the self.

So I took my

Precious body

To the ocean

Far away from

The castles and towers

That I had been

Walking towards

For so long

And my breath

Became mine

Again.

Here, I yield

Into the seat

Of my power

And expand

Into its beauty.

No longer

Door knocking

Or looking for ways

To infiltrate

Spaces or systems

That are not ready

For my specific

Kind of splendor.

Rather

Staying here

Speaking softly

To the wind

Letting her carry my voice

To the ears

Of the ones

Who are waiting

Ready for their invitations.

Permission to wait.

Hustle might work in business, but it never works in love. Since leaving Joseph a few years prior, I had entered hustle mode. I was an expert at making piles of shit look like castles of gold. While the outside world saw an independent women ascending in her career as a thought-leading therapist, I was in ride or die mode, holding up a fancy expat life in Singapore on a therapist's salary.

I'd been having issues getting a visa to stay in the country. Single mothers without much bank are not the most attractive candidates. But I was determined to stay. My career was just beginning to flourish, and my beautiful children were here. It wasn't an option to leave. But aside from paperwork problems, there was the question of money. I had to figure out how to pay rent, put food on the table and keep up with my expat wife friends who were largely funded by their hubbies with big jobs. The stress was real, and the implications of not being able to sustain this life were getting realer by the day. So, I worked, worked, worked.

I was used to hustle, having done it since leaving home at seventeen. Life was one big rolling hustle, until illness knocked on my door and took me off my feet for over a decade.

So, moving back into hustle mode was familiar territory.

But my hustle wasn't just a practical matter. It was part of me replaying my trauma story. Survival masked as skill. The quest for success feeding the lost little girl inside me who was craving the kind of validation that only daddies can give. That my daddy never gave. Still, the hard work was paying off.

The waitlist to see me as a client was growing.

More practitioners were working at my clinics.

I was getting more requests for speaking engagements.

My social media following was growing.

More, more, more.

Better, better, better.

My ego was drunk in the high altitudes of the mountain I was climbing.

I was hyper-productive. Outcome oriented. No goal too far or high for me to reach.

While my purpose to help people heal remained pure and true, the business and commercial side of things was like a snake slithering its way around my soul.

My philanthropic heart has always been at odds with my entrepreneurial spirit. I wished that I could disconnect my healing work from commerce altogether, but it was not possible.

I found myself knocking on bigger, more important doors, and getting them slammed in my face, or worse, standing there banging and banging with no reply. I was hungry for bigger contracts with larger organizations. It was partly about my ego climbing the invisible ladder and partly about earning more money to fund my increasingly expensive life.

In the world of entrepreneurship, there's sometimes a thousand no's before you reach one yes. And everything is a carefully crafted sale.

"You're a walking manipulation," my ex-husband said to me early in our marriage. It was one of those sudden comments that hits you right between the eyes and the truth is so uncomfortable that it's brushed off as a joke. Locked in the old trunk under the bed, never to be discussed again.

After a long slog of a week of meetings, sitting quietly with a cup of tea and my feet in a salty foot bath, while my children were zoned in on their precious forty-five minutes of iPad time, I found those old words swarming in the front of my head. To be honest, I wasn't really thinking about work, though I was feeling a little burnt out from pitches, meetings, podcasts and the one-on-one meetings with my team. I was thinking about my love life.

Surprise, surprise.

After a brief hiatus, I'd been back on the dreadful dating apps and had a series of seemingly difficult interactions. I'd seen Dylan a couple of times for coffee, but I wasn't excited enough by our connection to put energy into it. I was in this funny place that felt weirdly half-hearted and frustrating. Honestly, it felt like it was easier to grow a global business than find a boyfriend. I could strategize and sell my way into boardrooms or conference halls. But I couldn't strategize and sell my way into love. At least not healthy love.

When it came to the dating dance, I often stepped into a very performative, productive space. I was 'producing' dates and trying to lead the connection to the next step. I also didn't listen to boundaries; moments of honesty when men tried to let me know where and who they were. I was a fucking steamroller. It was all unconscious. Learned.

This tended to lead to one of two outcomes very quickly. Either I'd get involved with weak, pussy-footed men and find myself feeling resentful at their lack of direction, or I'd end up in some half-hearted dance with a man who was either still pining for his ex, dating around with his unconsidered dirty dick, or with a man who was clearly looking for his long-lost mummy dearest and desperate to play out some kind of avoidant control games.

When I paused to look at my part, I realized I needed to work on my control issues. To stop trying to paint a picture of what I wanted a dating scenario to look like and let it evolve. To let someone show me who they were and let invitations and reciprocity emerge… or not. This proved much easier said than done. Defragging deep-seated relational issues takes time, unlearning, relearning and course-correcting. It also takes a lot of humility, grieving and self-compassion. What was interesting was that here, I could clearly see the link between these patterns with men and my entrepreneurial life.

I knew I needed a big shift. To take a pause. Come out of hustle. Reset. Let go of control. Stop climbing the mountain. I hadn't had a real break in three years. So, after a therapy session (or three) with Tabitha, I decided to take a leap of faith and invest in myself. The idea of stepping off my track was so confronting. One of my biggest existential fears was that I'd end up homeless, mentally ill, and alone. Dead in a ditch. There was also a shame piece.

Without my career and growing acclaim, was I worth anything at all? Fear and shame. Shame and fear. I knew I needed to work through this if I was to find any real kind of peace. And if I was going to access the kind of softness and surrender that I already knew was lacking in my approach to my love life.

A month off the grid. No business development. No teaching programs. No podcast interviews. No growth. No agenda. No kids, thanks to the support of Joseph and his partner who had offered to hold the fort while I took an extended trip. Just a month in the Croatian sun. A few online clients a week. The ocean. And some deep conversations with my heaving heart.

Croatian Sun

I am not deranged dear

I am detangling

From the coffin

Of your world order.

No longer a zombie

Walking the earth

Or dulling my

Brilliance

With the next

Wave

Of pill-popping poison

Or drink laced with

Dissociation.

I am dancing, my darling

Coming alive under

The Croatian sun.

You call me crazy

Cradling in the

Straight jacket

Of your own

Fear.

This is me

Wildly alive.

Kali is the Hindu Goddess of Destruction. Kali is also a small fishing village on the Ugljan island, about 25 minutes via ferry from Zadar, Croatia. I'd been researching for a quiet place to stay in Europe, away from the noise, party, tourist or Instagramable vibes. And when I came across Kali, it seemed perfect. The reference to the Hindu goddess absolutely played into my choice. I'd learned to make most of my decisions by instinct and intuition led through symbols, signs and somatic impulses. Aside from being attracted to the quaint, quiet, off the grid quality, I was pulled by the idea of destroying my tendency to hustle, control, validation seek, and all those things I knew were some kind of loveless trap.

I rented an Airbnb about a five-minute walk up the hill from the rocky beach, with sea views, a glorious terrace adorned with grape vines and local fig trees all around. While the interior was low key shabby, the covered terrace graced with the cool ocean breeze was the perfect place for me to write, rest, meditate and take sanctuary from my hectic Singapore world.

When I got there, it took me a good few days to exit mainstream mode. As I lugged my green suitcases along the rough, uneven streets, in the scorching heat, I had a moment of panic. A month here? In the middle of nowhere? What had I done? I'd developed enough of a compassionate witness to talk myself down. "Let it unfold, Lena," I calmed myself. "This is going to be a process." And with that moment of self-compassion, my breath deepened, and I could feel myself taking in clean rich air. Sweet from the fruit of the nearby trees, and salty with the sea gently permeating the atmosphere.

There wasn't much on the island. A wooden beach bar, a fish shack and one higher end local tavern. There were a couple of mini marts that stocked the bare minimum and the one proper supermarket on the island was a decent hike away. I wasn't used to so little stimulus or activity. And as I left my suitcases in the living room and went out on to the terrace to survey my surrounds, big juicy tears began to drop from my eyes and my chest began to heave. This heaving heart of mine finally had space to start telling her stories. After a bit of a cry, I picked up my phone to call Ellen. She was often the first person I reached for when I felt vulnerable and alone.

"I don't know what I'm doing here," I sniffed.

"What are you talking about?" Ellen challenged. "You're there to reset, get some perspective and write your next book, aren't you?"

"Y-y-yes," I stammered.

"Just enjoy it, darling! This is a gift! There's zero to be upset about."

Ellen was my nearest and dearest friend, but sometimes she couldn't really understand the strange dark places I went to. While she'd gone through her fair share of pain and trauma as an adult, her childhood had been quite charmed, bestowed with the kind of stable love and support I could only dream of. And she still held an incredibly close relationship with her parents and sister. My specific kind of darkness was foreign to her.

Earlier in our relationship, I'd been triggered a few times when she'd met my melancholia with sternness or invalidation. It would cause me to shut down, disconnect and pull away for a while. However, as our friendship had evolved and deepened, she'd taken the time to learn my unique, complex heart and become so much softer and loving in my moments of existential distress. In turn, I had become far less bothered when she set a healthy boundary around my plump tears or poochy pouts and could receive them as a grounded call to honor my increasingly abundant reality.

"You're right, as usual. It's so beautiful here. I'm so grateful to be here."

"Found any hot Croatian men yet?" she asked.

"Not yet, but let me get settled and get in my bikini and go down to the beach bar. I'm sure that will change things," I laughed.

"Ok, sweetie, love you so much. Keep me posted. And remember, enjoy the gift you're in right now! Gotta go. Bye, bye, love you, bye," she signed off.

There was a bottle of prosecco waiting from the Airbnb host in the fridge, so I decided to pop it and toast to the gift of being here. As I took my first sip, my phone lit up with Charlie video calling.

"Hey, hey, my Kali Croatian Goddess! How's the place?" she sang.

"Hey, babe, it's stunning. I can't wait for you to come this weekend. It's super quiet though. It's going to be a far cry from the party scene in Dubrovnik."

Charlie had been DJing at a summer music festival in Dubrovnik. I'd researched Croatia, in part, because I knew she'd been there and the idea of a few days together during my trip felt both fun and comforting.

"Oh my goddess, good!" Charlie chimed. "The festival has been so intense and amazing. But I am totally ready for some deep chill. I hooked up with this DJ that I'd met in LA last year and then I totally fell in love with this super-hot gay dude for about a minute and spent 24 hours testing to see if he'd turn for me. He didn't. The sets have been wild, and I've danced my ass off. Ready to detox."

"This is the perfect place for it," I responded. "I can't wait to hear all your stories when you get here."

"It's going to be beautiful. I've pulled out a couple of my favorite goddess meditations for us to do aaaannnnd I'm bringing my Kali oracle cards. Kali in Kali. How powerful is that? Big love! I'll text you from the ferry terminal."

Charlie always made me smile. A little bit wild, a little bit woo. Reflecting two parts of me that I'd packed away a long time ago. I could feel them itching to get out to play and often through her embodied invitation, they did.

But first, I had five days to myself. I'd blocked my calendar so there were no clients, meetings or agenda of any kind. All there was to do was swim, sunbake, sleep, eat and repeat. And write... but only if I felt like it. I was practicing the art of purposeless, organic flow and creative patience. That patience piece continued to be hard for me. As I began to drop into the agendaless environment, I could feel my guilt start to rise.

How could I be so selfish as to take this time for myself?

How could I leave my children for so long?

How could I expect their dad to step up and in?

How could I enjoy myself when... insert basically any ridiculous thing you can think of.

Generations of mother guilt were looking me in the face. As were generations of deprivation guilt connected to my ancestors and the Holocaust.

As a Jewish woman, I held so much complex intergenerational trauma. I could feel these two specific threads, circling my energy field, like smoky suffocating ropes. For a moment, I had some kind of vision or semi-flashback to what may have been my ancestors being marched through a concentration camp to the gas chambers. This wasn't the first time the gas chambers had appeared in my waking trauma processing. Sometimes when I was in a steam room, I had to steady myself so as not to enter some past-life, intergenerational dissociative nightmare. But right now, this old complex guilt was trying to wrap me in its tentacles, and I needed to meet it... and tell it to fuck off.

"I have nothing to be guilty about. I am worthy of rest. I am worthy of pleasure. I am worthy of joy. I set myself free. And I set all my ancestors free with my embodiment of freedom, peace and play." I repeated this mantra to myself between sips of prosecco. For a split second, I wondered if I was crazy, and then I reminded myself firmly, that I was anything but. I was healing.

I repeated the mantra one more time and then let out a series of sobs and dirty coughs. It was as if I was metabolizing something ancient.... I knew the signature of such energy by now. I looked around the terrace and off to the ocean in the distance. Right. Time for a nap, and then maybe a swim. I swigged the last of the prosecco in the glass and lay down to a dreamy sleep. Kali was already working her magic. I could feel it.

After a few days coming down out of hustle culture and into the arms of the island, I could feel my nervous system settling. I was sleeping by ten and rising at six, in the ocean every morning and back in bed for a post-lunch siesta. Afternoons were a mix of walks, writing time or a second dose of sunbaking. My life in Singapore and all my problems felt far away.

I'd made the mistake of opening my social media a few times which triggered sharp stabs of anxiety and shame when I'd see everyone selling or celebrating their wins, on the climb of that familiar never-ending hill. It became quicker and quicker to course-correct my thinking from "I'm wasting time, I need to get back out there," to "Gosh, I am grateful for this beautiful life I have." On day four, the sense of gratitude became automatic, and I wasn't forcing rest; I was just resting. The shift was palpable. I was sure that by the time I left island, my nervous system would be reset.

Now that I was feeling more relaxed, I decided to see if I could apply this new-found surrender to the way I related with men. I put on my cutest strapless bikini top with little gold charms across the bust and a long black skirt with high slits and made my way down to the beach bar to see what flirting could be done with the locals.

Zero.

Zip.

Nada.

Nil.

After two hours and my third Aperol spritz, I was sweaty, bored and mildly cranky. I'd had zero luck. Aside from a sweet seventy-year-old fisherman who had showed me his cool box with seven fish he'd caught and gutted that day, I hadn't got any attention. This really wasn't a party island. And I'd chose it specifically for that reason... to rest and go inward.

"You're confusing the universe!" I heard Charlie's voice in my head. She's right, I was. Feeling frustrated and slightly stupid, I hopped off my bar stool, flung some euros on the table and climbed the lonely hill home.

The next morning, it was mid-swim that I realized even the act of perching myself at the bar looking cute was a kind of performative production. It was me trying to curate or conjure a situation, rather than let it happen. I shook my head with the realization and accidentally took a big gulp of sea water. Coughing and spluttering, I rushed to shore where I paused on my hands and knees to regain my breath.

"Here, take some water," offered a deep Croatian voice. In my distress, I didn't look up before I grabbed the bottle that had been passed to me and took a drink. Once I regained my composure, I lifted my head to see a tanned tall sandy-haired man in a boating uniform. The sun glistened behind his head like a halo.

"Hvala," I thanked him in Croatian.

"Don't mention it," he replied. "The winds just picked up a few minutes ago, so you can expect the sea to be a little rougher today. Stay safe." He offered me a hand to help me stand up, which I awkwardly took. "I'm Tommy. I'm a skipper on that boat over there." He pointed to a particularly lush catamaran about 50 feet away. "We don't have any clients for a few days, so we are having a small party tomorrow night. You should come. It starts at nine pm. Ok?"

"Ok," I said, stunned. "I'm Lena, by the way."

"It's a date then. See you," he confirmed, winked, and walked off.

That was quick, I thought. In the sea one moment, processing about how to stop producing my love life, and a meet-cute moment the next. The girls were going to love hearing about this.

I felt a bit nervous about going to the party alone, but I worked through it and turned up shyly in a long white semi-see-through dress over my leopard-print bikini at nine-thirty pm. It ended up being a good night, with a bit of wine, dancing and a sweet goodnight kiss from Tommy. There wasn't really a connection, but it was fun to spend the night in a playful and purposeless state. It offered me a certain kind of glow that was different to that sun-kissed feeling. It was a man-kissed feeling.

Two days later, Charlie flew in for the long weekend, and in the end, after I twisted her arm, Esther ended up flying in too. She'd been curating an event in Paris that blended photography and orchestral music, and I'd convinced her to extend her trip and come for a girl's weekend.

Over the next few days with the combined magic of our trio, divine love meditations, daily oracle card readings and at-home pedicures, there were many more moments of organic playful romance. I ended up dancing salsa by the beach with a Mexican dancer who was performing at a street show in a nearby village. Charlie, no stranger to the art of the threesome, spent the evening with two visiting Slovenian sailors and we coached Esther into flirting with a cute Croatian guy at the beach bar which culminated in her first post-split kiss.

Next to Charlie, I felt like a frigid novice, but next to Esther, I felt like a burlesque bad-ass. On our last night, we were up into the wee hours of the morning, swapping stories and setting intentions for the kind of love we wanted. As I drank in the joy of the weekend, I had a moment of that familiar guilt rise. Neither of these other women were mothers. I had children at home. How could I be here acting like a silly teenager? Shouldn't I be home brushing my daughter's hair, or working hard to save for their university fees?

I took a breath and caught myself.

This was all part of it. I'd been so busy being what the world wanted me to be, what I was told I should be. Producing a burnt-out out bossy version of myself that didn't really make me happy or take me towards the kind of love I craved or really the kind of life I wanted at all. "I'm right where I'm meant to be," I whispered to myself. Learning to live.

Immaculate Humanity

When I step

Fully off

My track

And come into

Presence

Service

All my stories

Disappear.

My heart

Opens wide

My fascia

Softens

So, I can receive you

Just as you are.

In your

Immaculate

Humanity.

Seeing.

You.

Love.

When we are not wading through a complex competitive world, it's natural that we will soften, open our hearts and begin to see through a purer lens.

As my nervous system detoxed, my heart softened. After two weeks on the island in Croatia, I found myself feeling relaxed, with a new kind of warmth and sparkle emitting from my eyes and skin every day. There was nothing to brace against, reach for, manage, build or navigate. I was off my 'track' and living in line with the sun, the moon, the ebb and flow of the tides and the natural impulses of my body.

It was like I'd taken my capitalist survival glasses off and was seeing clearly for the first time in a long time. I could feel so much more space inside me. All this extra capacity and growing grace came in handy when Leonardo suddenly re-entered my life.

I'd just returned from a hike, poured myself some cool aloe vera drink and sat down to check my phone. It had been three years since our last interaction, and there it was. A text message from his Italian number.

Mermaid... I have been thinking about you a lot recently. It's been a hell of a few years and you're on my mind. I miss you. X

Funnily enough, I had been thinking about Leonardo a few days prior. His image had popped up in one of my meditations and it was also around the same time of year that I had ended it with him. I'd had a bit of a cry about it.

Since him, no one had really touched my heart in the same way or made me orgasm as delightfully and deliciously.

I find it interesting how our inner world can wonderfully emerge in our outer world with such synchronicity from time to time. I always take these moments as little signs of alignment, embodiment or 'meant to be'. It feels like more than coincidence.

The moment I read the text, my confused heart both expanded and contracted, beating loudly with many desires and fears surfacing. Oh, how I wanted this man. To feel his big strong arms around me, to feel so safe with my back arched over them. I'd fantasized about our sex life many, many times on lonely nights in. But along with the intense desire came intense fear.

I was terrified of getting hurt. It had taken so much to end things with him. He held some kind of dangerous power over me. In his presence, I was his. Totally abandoned. But he wasn't really available to hold me, not emotionally or practically. It's as if I could feel the impending betrayal, discard and mammoth heartbreak he could cause. And I didn't like that he hadn't been one hundred percent honest with me from the beginning about how entwined in his marriage he was. I don't do married men. It's a rule. And his lack of honesty had caused me to breach my own ethical code. Once I was hooked, it was so hard to reinstate it, and I didn't until I could feel he really had the power to smash my heart into a million pieces.

While I had said goodbye to him in a loving and grown-up way, I realized I was clearly still holding some resentment about how things had started and a splinter of heart-pain around having to give up a man I so thoroughly enjoyed. As my thoughts swirled, and my heart continued to boom inside me, I was able to realize that I was not feeling clear about the situation, so I decided to pause and find equilibrium before responding to him.

The pre-Croatia version of me would have sent back some sassy, semi "come hither" kind of reply that would have either pushed him away or found myself right back in bed with him, primed for eventual heart break.

Over the evening, I allowed my thoughts to come and go and detangle. In the space, several things became clear to me: First, I was pleased he had reached out. In fact, I'd kind of been dreaming about reconnecting. Maybe this was some kind of psychic manifestation. Second, he hadn't really done anything wrong aside from omitting information during a couple of casual sexcapades. We were both complicit in continuing once I knew he was ensconced in unfinished business with his ex. I acknowledged that three years is a long time. If I had changed (which I really had), maybe he and his circumstances may have changed too? I could also feel that my desire to shut it down was entirely self-protective, as it was when I ended it three years ago. And finally, I was far wiser, more grounded and discerning now, and if I did connect or go to bed with him, I trusted my ability to look after my heart.

With these clear, grounded thoughts was also the part of me that wanted to fly into the fantasy that he was single and ready to hold my heart. The hope that we would live happily ever after in an international romcom kind of fairytale. Yep, I totally had that going on. But even being able to look at it allowed me not to get lost in it.

After rewriting the message about twelve times to find the right balance of interest and nonchalance, I replied, *Hey Leo... it's been a while. You've been on my mind too... what's new?*

We exchanged a few texts and the moment I let him know I was in Croatia for a month, he responded. *I want to come to you, Mermaid. It's no coincidence we happen to be so close right now.*

The idea of a visit triggered my internal alarm bell system... as well as made my pants wet. Oh, my goodness. Should I say yes, or shut this shit down tight? I needed a hot minute to think.

If I'm honest, I knew I'd let him come to visit me on the island. Even if I fooled myself that I needed to think about it and might not. I chose not to chat about it with my girlfriends, which was unusual for me. Normally, I needed Ellen and Charlie to play their roles as angel and devil, whispering their opinions in my ears. But I knew this little girl game would confuse me further. I decided to follow my impulse. Whether healthy or destructive, this meeting was meant to be.

He met me at the local beach bar on a Friday afternoon. I was wearing a plunging floral one piece and flowy blue pants as well as a wide brimmed hat. My hair was wavy from the salt and my skin was the perfect kind of sun-kissed from two weeks on the island. As I approached the bar, I saw him sitting there in his crisp white shorts and pale pink linen top, the first few buttons undone, so I could get a glimpse of his inviting chest, the corner of that shag-alicious wolf tattoo, just visible. His hair was longer than when I'd last seen him.

He looked good. So good. I could feel my heart flutter, and I reminded myself of my intention. *Just let him show you who he is and where he is, no expectation, no purpose, no stories. Just let him be a man*, I coached myself. I had a tendency to cast men into roles and wanted to see if I could not do that here, my point for personal inquiry.

"Lena, you're even more stunning than I remember. How is that possible?" he flirted.

This was so Leonardo. He could charm the pants off anyone in thirty seconds flat. Or less. I noticed a hint of that same blend of expansion and contraction that I'd felt when he had reached out. The desire was still the same, but the contraction actually felt like a whiff of judgmental anger.

You're such a fucking womanizer, it silently spoke. I caught it, drew a circle around it and sent it up to the locked box of "shit to process later." I softened my hips and flashed a coy smile. "It's good to see you, Leo. I like the pink on you."

He ordered me a wine spritzer and gazed at me with masculine desire. And we sat like that silently, looking at each other for about two minutes. I couldn't tell if it was foreplay or a power game. Maybe a bit of both. Finally, he broke the silence and asked me to fill him in on the last few years. I gave him a very topline impersonal overview and indicated it was his turn to share.

"I just filed for divorce two weeks ago," he blurted, "so I wanted to see you."

The news pierced the bubble of my inexpertly held complex thoughts and in that moment, it was as if I had no way to process the information at all. I just knew I wanted him. Now.

"Good to know," I managed to reply. "I'm going for a swim." I expertly slid off my blue pants and slunk across the bar, down the steps into the cool Adriatic Sea.

I swum around the corner of the bar to a little alcove, to get a bit of breathing room. Why was he here? Did he want to get back together or just a raunchy weekend? Why after all this time? I could feel myself entering a mild panic. I tried to regulate my breathing. "Remember, Lena," I told myself, "Stay present, stay purposeless."

As I soothed myself, he appeared in front of me, a merman coming to find his mermaid mate. I had so many memories in the ocean with this hunk of a man. Our favorite date day had been to head out on a boat on the water and sip prosecco, swim, kiss and lay in the sun. Surely once more couldn't hurt.

Without words, he wrapped one arm around my back and used his leg to hitch mine up around his waist. He pressed his mouth on mine, and I was back in the dynamic paradise we seemed to effortlessly co-create. It was a deep kiss, full of passion, but also full of pain. When he pulled away, I felt like he had telepathically told me so many stories. Downloaded through his kiss, through his embrace. His eyes held a certain tenderness. I could tell he had been through hell and back. I decided not to broach it for the moment, and we stayed in the water, without speaking, just swimming, kissing and being in what felt like our natural habitat. It was as if we had perhaps had some past life together here. It was a remembering.

Later, we went back to my apartment and simply lay together. He didn't rip my clothes off as I had expected (and perhaps wanted) him to. Instead, he lay across from me, looking into my eyes, and occasionally reached out to stroke my hair, or trace the arc of my shoulder or breast. Every cell in me was alive with lust, but I just lay there, listening, receptive. I knew he had a story to tell me. And he did.

He told me of some very psychologically abusive behavior from his wife, the threat of having his children taken from him and the level of financial blackmail that had been going on. As I quietly listened to his story, I could see this beautiful and destroyed man. In his immaculate humanity. Trying to do his best. Failing. Navigating the torture of love gone wrong. It's always messy. He had a long road ahead of him. It was likely going to be a year or two of legal battles and restoring his sovereignty.

There was something powerful about seeing him in his honest vulnerability for me. While a part of me yearned for him, another part of me could clearly see he in no way had the capacity to love me well. At least not right now. It's as if I was back in the same conundrum as three years ago. I had been at this particular juncture many times. And in the past, I tended to either get lost in the oxytocin rush and lean into pleasure, and eventual hurt, or I'd run so far, locking my heart up in a box and shutting my legs tight. In both scenarios, the man would be a perpetrator, either past or potential. Spiritually, it felt like this curve in the healing spiral was asking me to do this differently. To let him be just a man, to love him, and to let him go… without judgement, label or categorization. And so, I did.

We made the most tender love all night long. And I could feel myself continuing to flick between wanting to push him away and clinging on tight, imagining our happily ever after together. I stopped myself each time and returned to the lines of his body, the scent of his skin. Sweat and salt mixed with cologne. Returned to our breath. Our rhythm. Our moment of shared humanity.

The next morning, I told him, "Leo, you have the most special spot in my heart. No man has touched me the way you have. I'm so glad you reached out. But I also see we are back where we began. You, reaching for me, yet not ready to hold my heart. I don't want to get involved right now. But I want to stay connected. Maybe one day you will be ready to love me. I'm not going to wait around. But I do want to keep the door open."

He replied by kneeling on the floor, taking my hands and kissing them, almost bowing or praising my mini monologue. I could see he was holding back tears. I cupped the left side of his face in my hand and drew him up to stand before me. "You're the most special woman, Mermaid," he spoke softly. "You're right."

In that moment, I felt such love between us. Such recognition of what could not be. A living bittersweet symphony. We made love one more time, then he showered and left. Watching him walk away felt hard but necessary. As soon as I closed the door, I burst into tears. The kind of ugly cry that most commonly happens in solitude. I stamped my foot, snot pouring down my face, and I flung myself on my bed, hugging a pillow that still smelled like him, like our sex, for comfort. Once I calmed down, I took a long shower to cool and cleanse. I lay on my yoga mat and chose an energy healing playlist on Spotify. It felt like a huge growth moment on the road to love.

To see. To love. To let go. To keep doors open. I lay there feeling soft, sincere and sad. "You're unlocking your heart, Lena," I whispered to myself. "Keep going."

Pussy Whips

My heart opened

So wide

And I couldn't

Tolerate it

So I clamped it down

Fast and hard.

And then I lost you.

I was trying

To keep it open

But all my

Sleeping sisters

Urged me to enter

Their trance.

Conditioned

To demand

More

Hide my cooch

Under rose petals

And build

An obstacle course

Around me.

Make him come to you.

He needs the chase.

Don't give it to him so easy.

Respect yourself.

And perhaps

They did

Lure some men

Into nuptials

Who rode

White horses

And offered

Treasure chests

Of gold.

And perhaps

They sat

In chariots

And took

Pretty pictures

Checked off

Long lists.

But I could see

The tails

Of their whips

Peeking out

From under their

Petticoats.

And the faint smell

Of burnt souls

Steam coming out

Those princes'

Ears

And the stiff footsteps

They left behind them

Pussy-whipped.

I never wanted

To turn you

Into a handcuffed

Prince

My love.

I'm sorry

I listened

To the collective

And barricaded

Myself up tight.

I've been untying

The knots

Around my heart

So I can

Open to you

Once more.

And I'm terrified.

Learning to love you

Freely

Seeing what it's like

To meet you

In this field

Of flowers.

No bricks

To build

Or road to walk.

No suffering

No silence

No sneaky

Agenda

No whips.

A beating heart

A pussycat

And my messy

Golden hair.

And you.

Ten rules to catch a husband. About six weeks after returning from Croatia, I was sitting at a women's networking lunch in Singapore listening to a bunch of women in power suits talk about the connection between sex and the boardroom. A curious combination. I was there to listen and learn. It was one of those female empowerment events I tended to stay far away from, but this one had me interested. The purpose was to unlock the women's leadership potential, but the conversation around the room mostly went to love, sex and romance. Just the topic I was exploring. Their marriages, their divorces and their part time lovers around the world. It all felt so alpha. So male. So manipulative. This is how I 'hooked' my husband.

Later that week, I was sitting by my pool with about ten mothers from school as the kids swam and I felt the same energy of female trickery and power. "I made him come to me." "He bought me a fifty-thousand-dollar diamond... and only then did I sleep with him." It felt like love and partnership was just a game. While the mothers sipped their prosecco and cackled about their romantic wins, I entered a little trance of my own. Many moments of being told how to behave when it comes to love, sex, and dating flashed through my mind.

There was the lock him down tight kind. And then there was the don't settle for less than you deserve kind. Sometimes, it was hard to tell one from the other.

Don't have sex till after commitment.

Play hard to get. Make him come to you.

Don't double message.

Don't say "I love you" first.

Don't let him see you cry.

Don't put all your eggs in one basket. Keep your options open.

Don't let him have your heart too quickly.

Don't show too much cleavage. You'll give the wrong message.

Men date sexy, but they marry classy.

High collars and pearls signal "wife material" to the male unconscious (can you believe that one of the school mums had actually said this to me?!) I was more of a cleavage and rubies kind of woman, anyway.

Flashes of my mother, my auntie, my sister, Ellen, Charlie, Naomi, Esther, pearls, corsets, whips, chains, Alice in Wonderland following that cheeky rabbit down the rabbit hole of love. Everyone had an opinion on how to snare a stud. But when I paused and thought about it, none of the voices I had been listening to had the kind of relationship I was craving, calling in.

Sometimes, I was so sure the kind of relationship I was holding out for was possible, that I'd eventually find it. But other times, I found myself feeling hopeless, wondering if I should settle for some lack-luster love, or one that was part of the old patriarchal patterns that were mirrored back to me daily. When I'd enter this head space, I'd usually end up attracting and dating some dude I knew wasn't what I really wanted, feeling frustrated, but at least, somewhat... occupied.

On this occasion, I decided to direct my energy to my own processing and to gather more information. Was there really a formula to find a mate, or was this a load of femme fatale power games? I decided to hold a girls' night at my place, specifically to explore this topic with my crew. Why not pair a bit of bonding time with some much-needed research?

I knew that Naomi was flying into town for a meeting later in the month, so I decided to time the event so the five of us could be together in person, instead of tapped in via Zoom. Ellen, Esther and Charlie were all coming. Our girls' nights had become a semi-regular thing through Covid. We would meet online with drinks in hand, snacks at the ready to check in, show support, have a giggle and remedy our loneliness. Post-Covid, we hadn't been as regular, with the world opening up and our lives back to their fast-paced international flow. I did miss our catch-ups. As women, we wove a magical net to hold and guide each other through life. And staying connected was important for making sure that none of us ever fell through the cracks that deepen through absence.

My matriarchal, entertainer energy was on full display as I prepared for the evening. I loved to host in my home. This time, I hung red Japanese lanterns on my balcony and had vases of white and purple orchids everywhere as well as every candle I could find. I'd gathered origami paper left over from a recent workshop and some pens. It was going to be a Japanese feast along with deep inquiry and story-telling all about love. I'd prepared a series of questions, but I knew that as soon we got into the vibe of the evening, it would flow organically. Staying in theme, I dressed up in a beautiful red silk kimono and swept my hair in a high bun and applied my favorite red lipstick. I loved any reason to get glammed up.

As the girls arrived, I offered them a choice of sake or an elderflower and lychee mocktail punch I'd made. Naomi arrived first. I'd planned a little extra time with her before the others arrived so I could catch up on the latest wedding news. She shared how her mother was very disapproving of her love match and had a bit of a cry. She'd spent years being the good Indian daughter and really tried to make the whole arranged marriage thing work. Now that she'd finally found love on her terms, she just wanted her mother to offer her blessing.

"She's being so mean," Naomi blubbered. "She will barely talk to me, and when she does, all she does is shame me, tell me I am a bad daughter, and that I will be sorry. It's awful."

"You're not a bad daughter, darling," I attempted to comfort her. "You are breaking barriers to claim the love you deeply want. It's brave. It's beautiful. Your mum can't understand your path, and that must feel… heart wrenching."

"It really does," Naomi affirmed. "But I keep reminding myself that I am choosing love. And I really have found it, Lena. He's just the best man I've ever met. I love him so much."

"I am so, so, so, so happy for you. And I am so proud of you too, Nai. I can't wait to celebrate you both soon." I wiped the tear off her cheek and embraced her, adding in an extra squeeze so she could really feel it.

Shortly after, the others began to arrive and we found ourselves sitting on my beautiful balcony, eating, laughing and dipping into some deep conversation about how to attract a partner.

Naomi shared a little with the group about the conditioning she had grown up with. Be a good girl. Be quiet. Close your legs. Do as you're told. Smile sweetly. Calm him down when he is angry. Don't blame him. He's the provider and what he says goes. Be grateful when he shows small moments of kindness.

"I honestly felt like I was being turned into a doll with a stitched-up mouth, and after a while, I couldn't handle it anymore. The thing is, my parents have a great marriage.

It worked for them. And from their generation there are so many examples where matchmaking works. Of course, there are plenty of matches that are an absolute mess. Sometimes you can see it from the moment the wives start shrieking at their husbands, or when he sends her an icy stare to be quiet. And sometimes, you hear about it through the grapevine, but in person, they put on a great front. It honestly felt so confusing to break away from it because I know it can and does work. A couple of my childhood friends found great matches and are recently married. One of them is pregnant. The thing is... it just didn't feel right for me."

I could feel Charlie's body bracing with anger as she listened to Naomi's story. "No-one has the right to tell you how to love, or even how to find love. God, that's some fucked up shit! So proud of you, babe, for saying no to such archaic nonsense!"

Esther, ever the equalizer, could sense the energy rising in the room, and Naomi's discomfort with Charlie's well-meaning but somewhat culturally insensitive and brash retort. "You know, everything has a time and place. Perhaps arranged marriage worked in certain cultures at a different time. Our world has changed so much in the last few decades. Women are claiming their voices and their power. We are far more inter-cultural than ever before, far more worldly, independent and our expectations for partnership keep getting higher." She was Chinese-Australian and had her own complex cultural conditioning to navigate. "You know, I think I married my mother," she said. We all burst into fits of laughter. "It's true, it's true. Look, my mother was such a distressed and volatile creature. I think she was so oppressed and unhappy, and it came out as her being emotionally reactive, shaming and blaming us behind doors, but putting on a front of the perfect Chinese wife in public. I learned to people please, keep her happy, or at least minimize her distress. It was never about me or my sisters. The whole house revolved around Mum's moods. Fast forward, at eighteen I chose a man who was just like her. Perfect gentleman in public, but behind closed doors, passive aggressive, emotionally reactive, and I ended up basically being his emotional sponge or soother... or something like that. I totally lost myself in that marriage. Fifteen years of it. You know what else? I think I became my dad in the process. Stoic. The caretaker. Never make a fuss. In some ways normalizing my partner's distress, maybe even enabling it."

We all nodded, seeing what she was saying.

She continued, "The reason my marriage went south was because I started speaking up, setting boundaries, taking up more space. And he couldn't handle it. It's like my honest existence made him mad or made him feel like I didn't love him enough."

"Mummy issues," I chimed in.

We all broke into fits of hysterical laughter again... each one of us familiar with the kind of men that want to turn us into their unloving mothers.

"So, how's it going now as you start to date, Esther?" Ellen asked. "Are you learning to take up more space?"

Esther paused. "Oh my god, one step at time, Ellen! I'm learning how to put lipstick on for the first time in ten years. I think before I learn to take up more space, I also have to learn to stop controlling, leading and planning everything. I realize that the moment I start chatting to a man, I want to choose the restaurant, book the table and make sure things run well. And I'm not sure that's the right energy to bring."

"You're totally in your masculine, honey," piped up Charlie, who'd been looking on, unusually quiet. While the rest of us in the group had either been or were about to be married, Charlie had chosen the path of 'single by choice,' so her views on partnership held a different quality.

"What do you mean?" asked Esther. "I'm not masculine."

"Leading is masculine. If you're in your feminine, you wait for them to come to you. Let them take the lead and plan. But to be honest, I think the conversation needs to go even deeper. Why are you all worried about how to get and keep a guy in the first place?"

The energy in the room shifted gears. We had gone from unpacking our conditioning, to questioning the desire for partnership all together.

"Life is just better with a mate," Ellen replied flatly. "Look, I know about being single. I know about being a single mother. I did it for years. At some point, we all want to lean into relationship. To be loved, supported. To be pleasured. There is absolutely nothing wrong with wanting partnership or marriage."

You could feel the line of tension between Ellen and Charlie. Charlie challenging marriage, and Ellen cheerleading it.

As was often her deeply conscious way. Charlie paused and found her center and compassionate voice. "You're right, Ellen. There's nothing wrong with wanting partnership and marriage. But there is also nothing wrong with not wanting it at all. Or at least not wanting to play into the old programs around courtship, contracts and the idea of eternity. Don't get me wrong, I love love. But I don't want to feel like I have to be a certain way to get a guy or commit to the idea of ever after."

All our heads bobbed up and down in agreement.

"That's the bit I really wanted to explore tonight," I expressed. "You know I am dying to meet my guy. And that I have this vision of conscious love, whatever the hell that means. But I keep noticing that whenever groups of women are talking about dating, sex and romance, they are prescribing almost steps or ways of approaching it that seem either totally self-abandoning or like some game. Even you, Charlie, have told me to play it cool or pull back. Isn't that a game? And

Ellen, you've told me plenty of times to close my legs until commitment. Isn't that a game too? I'm curious to learn if there is any formula to follow, or are all our rules making it worse?"

The silence was thick with process and reflective tension. Everyone was in deep thought around my question.

Naomi broke the silence. "Coming from a paradigm laced with rules, I say fuck them all."

"Cheers to that, Nai! And cheers to your engagement. And cheers to love without rules," I replied.

Whatever threads of conflict that had risen in our group dissipated and the room filled with celebration.

I liked the idea of love without rules. I wondered what would happen if I began to date without any rules at all.

Improv

I am not ready

To roll out

The red carpet

To my heart

Or to plant the garden

That will

Feed us

When the world

Implodes.

I'm not ready

To write

The story

Where you're my

Co-star

And the ending is

Tied up

All nice and neat.

I want to live

In a choose your own

Adventure

For a while

Where we

Weave

In and out

Of chapters

Not knowing

When we will

Next meet.

Welcoming beautiful

Surprises

Choices

Impulses

And leaps

Into shared

Moments

And memories.

Meet me here

My love

In the adventure

So that if we

Choose

To write

An epic

Romance novel

Together

Theres's context

Ground

Muscle memory

Themes

Shared vision.

For now

Be my improv

Partner

Play with me.

All great inventions begin here.

Sometimes we think we want something, and then when we get it, we realize we don't want it at all.

I'd been casually dating Dylan, the Swedish operations guy I'd met at the beach. While things hadn't initially sparked, we'd stayed in touch and something felt different with him once I was back from Croatia. Our coffee catch-ups transitioned to semi-regular dates. When I was in town, we'd see each other once a fortnight. And while my pants weren't exploding with fireworks, it was all quite lovely. Regulated. Consistent. There was no uncertainty. Total responsiveness. Resect. Playfulness. Weirdly, I hadn't had sex with him. We'd go to dinner, or on a picnic or hike and each date would end with a sweet kiss goodbye. The hottest we got was one evening after a Cabaret show when we ended up on my couch with a bottle of wine and my breasts in his mouth. But it hadn't gone any further. I didn't want it to.

Usually, I couldn't wait to get naked. I had such a high libido, and once I felt a connection, didn't wait long to consummate it. With Dylan, something told me to hold back. I wasn't sure if it was because I wasn't so attracted to him (though he was a good looking man, so it didn't really make sense) or if I was playing some unconscious game, trying to be potential partner material (though that didn't feel true either). I was a little perturbed by my out of character behavior.

One evening, about ten dates in, Dylan, in his relaxed no fuss way said to me: "Lena, I think it is time we talked about exclusivity."

Taken off guard, I squirmed in my seat. "Why? We are not even sleeping together," I retorted, immediately embarrassed.

"I know, but I'd like to go there with you, and I think commitment beforehand is important. Don't you?"

I'd been seeking commitment with a man for ages, and it had always felt elusive. Yet here, when it was being handed to me,

I found my body contracting. It was saying no, no, no loud and clear.

"I don't think I am ready, Dylan. It's a big step." He looked hurt momentarily and then his Swedish suit of armor covered it up. I reached to touch his arm. "We can talk more about it," I said tenderly. "Can you give me some time to think about it all? I want to get clear. I have therapy on Tuesday. I'll talk it over with Tabitha. How about dinner Tuesday night?"

"Sure, we can do that," he replied graciously.

The rest of the evening felt somewhat disconnected, and though I tried to bridge the gap, I could feel Dylan had pulled back, to protect his heart.

I was baffled by my response.

"What's wrong with me?" I exclaimed to Tabitha in session the following week as I recounted the story.

"Stop doing that, Lena. Stop self-pathologizing. You're having a valid response to the idea of exclusivity with Dylan. Your body's talking to you."

"But commitment is what I have been craving!" I whined. "And here's this nice dependable man who's showing up for it and my body can't get on board! I'm so frustrated."

"Well, what's your body telling you?"

I closed my eyes and put my hand on my heart, tuning in. "I'm not ready." The message was clear. "I don't understand why I am not ready. I *am* ready."

"Not according to your body," Tabitha said. "The question is, why are you not ready? Is it that you need more time to feel safe with him? Are you afraid of commitment? Are you not sure you're that into him?"

"I'm worried he's not the right guy for me. I'm afraid of being trapped. I got lost in my marriage. And I can see with him it would move fast. And I just need to slow it down."

"Then you have your answer. It's perfectly okay to admit that you have these fears. That you aren't yet truly emotionally available for commitment."

"Fuck, Tabitha, you're right. I'm not emotionally available."

This was news to me. I'd been so used to attracting emotionally unavailable men and thought they were the problem. But the moment I met an emotionally available man, it highlighted my own unavailability. I was floored with the truth staring at me in the mirror. I wasn't ready to be in a relationship.

"So, what do I do now?" I asked Tabitha.

"Be honest with him. That's the pathway to intimacy, regardless. Let him know what you are and aren't available for. And invite him to do the same."

"Okay, let's see what happens. I'll update you next week."

I gulped the rest of my licorice tea and left the room. I went to the restroom to touch-up my makeup in the mirror. As I layered on my newest lip-gloss, I looked back at my emotionally unavailable eyes in the mirror. They filled with shame and then welled with grief. I wanted to be emotionally available. I was the problem here. It was me. I know Tabitha was encouraging me to stop self-blaming and shaming, but I honestly felt like a fuck-up. But I caught myself and softened my gaze. "Ok, Lena," I said to my reflection, "we have more healing work to do." I took a breath and turned to walk down the street and catch a taxi to meet Dylan for dinner.

As usual, he had booked an excellent restaurant and was waiting to greet me, kiss both my cheeks and pull out my chair, a total gentleman. After a bit of small talk, he inquired, "So, how was therapy?"

It was my cue to get raw and real with him. "Dylan, I'm enjoying dating you, so much, and I don't want to stop. But I am not ready for exclusivity. It's not that I want to sleep with other people—I'm not sleeping with anyone actually—but my freedom is really important to me." He frowned, clearly not liking what he was hearing. So, I went on. "I lost myself in my marriage and I am scared of that happening again. I know I have some healing to do, but I just want to take it slow with no pressure. Would that be okay for you?" In the pause I blurted as an afterthought, "We can even start having sex."

He sat, trying to find the right words for a while. He'd open his mouth, then close it again, then pause, process and begin again. I tried to give him the space to formulate his thoughts, but my gut said, it wasn't going to be "Sure Lena, let's do it your way."

When he finally spoke, he reached and took my hand first. "What you're telling me makes absolutely sense, Lena. You have every right to date without commitment. The thing is, I don't know if I'm built like that. When I'm in, I'm in. So, we are in different places right now, it seems."

"I want to be in," I whispered, "but I am just not there yet. Could we just date for a few more months... and see?"

"I don't think that will work for me," he replied. I could feel the boundary was set, and this was the end. My throat clenched, holding back tears. "You are a special woman, Lena. It's been a pleasure dating you. But I think we need to end things here."

I nodded in agreement.

He signaled for the bill. "Let me at least drive you home, make sure you are safe and sound."

"Thank you," I agreed.

We drove home silently, neither of us daring to speak a word into the ravine that opened between us.

He walked me to my door, cupped my face in his hands and kissed me with delicate care.
"Take care, Lena. Perhaps another time, another place." I smiled, and he turned and disappeared into the night.

As soon as I got in the door, I bawled my eyes out. He was such a good guy. Why did I have to be so not ready for him? I could feel my inner-shame-blame-monster bitch rearing her angry head and said to myself, "It's okay, Lena, this is part of your journey. It's okay to want to take time to get to know someone. It's okay to still be healing. Better to go slow than leap into something you're not sure about."

Even my self-compassionate affirmations couldn't stop me from getting lost in the shame spiral. I flopped onto the couch under my favorite pink blanket and sobbed for a while, then called Ellen, who I knew would be the cheerleader I needed in that moment.

"He's not your guy, love," she offered. "You weren't ever that excited about him. You told him you needed time. He didn't want to give you time. And that's his choice for sure, but if he were your guy, he'd give you time. It's just not a match. I'm sorry."

"When am I going to find my match then?" I blubbered.

"Girl, you're on the journey. Love is a miracle. It doesn't happen every day. But you keep putting yourself out there. He's out there, I promise. And you need to casually date to get to know someone. That's smart. That's how you protect your heart. Don't let any guy rush you. When it's right, you'll know."

"Thanks, Ellen," I sniffed. "Dinner next week?"

"Sure, let's try that new Japanese place at Holland Village," she responded. "In the meantime, take care of your heart. Love you."

After a few days of wallowing, I came out of my post 'ending it with a nice guy' slump and realized that both Tabitha and Ellen were right. My body had been giving me clear messages not to lean in with Dylan. Whether it was a lack of chemistry, or a fear of commitment, or a bit of both didn't really matter. I needed to learn to trust my instincts.

And for me, it was important to truly get to know someone before committing to a relationship. And I wanted one, I really did. But I wanted to be smarter this time. Slower. More discerning. No rush, no force, no pressure or promises that simply couldn't be kept. Even though I was now man-less, perhaps I really was on the road to my healthy ever after, after all.

Poly

Poly wants a cracker

They're hungry

And the village bakery

Is out of bread.

Poly wants a tasting plate

Why commit to one main course

When you can have everything

On the menu.

Poly wants to pay the rent

Cost of living is high

And more mouths to feed

Sound the siren of survival.

Poly wants to process

They're still spinning

The same stories that their

Inner child hasn't integrated.

Poly wants to self-protect

They talk of free love

But really they're building walls

Around their tattered heart.

Poly seeking poly

All the empowered folks

Who've had enough of a system

Where love leaves us

Broken or broke.

Smart Poly

Scared Poly

Spread your wings, Poly (or your legs)

Redesigning love.

To poly, or not to poly, that was the question.

After recounting my ending with Dylan to Charlie, she'd suggested I explore the ENM (ethically non-monogamous) or 'poly' scene. She said it was the perfect way for me to get my dose of connection, some good orgasms, and remain attachment free. I'd always thought of myself as a monogamous kind of person but based on what happened with Dylan, I wasn't really ready for commitment. I decided try it out.

Charlie had flung herself full force into the world of secret sex parties, swinger's clubs and ethical non-monogamy. She'd often have four or five men she was sleeping with and was always beaming with that 'I've just had a bunch of great orgasms' kind of glow. I wanted some of what she was having... or did I? While I was attracted to the idea of connection, sex and freedom, I was also repelled by the idea of having multiple partners and for sex to be a given or an expectation. Something about that didn't sit right with me and made me contract into myself. Was I some kind of prude?

I was chatting about it to Esther one Monday. We'd started getting together every Monday evening for Vietnamese food and yin yoga, and each week we would share the round up of our dating life.

"I need a connection," Esther said clearly. "I can't just have sex with someone on command."

"Me neither," I stated. "But, oh my goodness, I'm so sexually frustrated at the moment. I would like to dip my toe in and see if I can open up and be more playful with it all. I feel like a fucking prude."

Esther broke into a fit of laughter. "You? A prude? You've got a new guy every other week and having little love affairs all over the world. You're the least prudish person I know. If you're a prude, I'm a dried-up old prune."

We both exploded into giggles and everyone in the restaurant looked at us. I lowered my voice a little. "You know I am dying to meet a partner, but I wonder if I need to work this out of my system first. Maybe it will help me become more emotionally available?"

"Look, I think that's a reach," Esther replied, "but if you want to explore, why not? Meanwhile, I'm practicing sitting across dinner tables, staring at suits, and trying not to yawn while men mansplain the most boring things to me, hoping I'll get a goodnight kiss if I smile enough."

"There's a sex party happening this Saturday. Charlie sent me the info. Come with us?"

"I don't know, that is so far out of my comfort zone," stammered Esther.

"Mine too!" I said. "Please, please, please be my wing woman? If it's horrible, we can leave."

"I'll come for an hour, max," replied Esther. "To be a supportive friend. But what do you wear to something like that?"

"Let's get dressed at my place and have prosecco beforehand. I'll ask Charlie if she wants to join too. Saturday, seven pm. We better scoot to yoga now though."

Through that evening's yoga class as I slid into the yin poses, I could feel my body tingling with excitement about the up-and-coming sex party. And a little bit of fear. That night when I went to sleep, I dreamed of being dressed in cream lace with a gorgeous green feathered and sequined masquerade mask on and having a delicious man with a black cat eye mask and leather black plants and no shirt, tracing my body with a long black feather. It was tantalizing, exciting and had me wake up ready for some self-pleasure time before getting on with my day. I was getting exhilarated at the thought of Saturday night's adventure. Maybe I could do the poly ENM sex party thing. Not such a prude after all.

My fantasy was a wild mismatch from reality.

When we entered the sex party, the scent of salty pleasure wafted in the air around us. The house was filled with music and semi-naked bodies moved in and out of rooms that were erupting with groans, grunts and cries of ecstasy. Where was my hot leather pants man from my dream earlier in the week? No fucking where to be seen.

Upon entry, we were asked to choose a colored wrist band to indicate our engagement levels. It was a cool safety signal. Green for "bring it on!", orange for "curious" and red for "just looking, don't touch me." Charlie chose green (of course), I opted for orange and after a pensive pause, Esther chose red.

"Bye, ladies, have fun!" Charlie skipped off to join one of the group orgy rooms, as she'd kindly told us she'd do in the taxi on the way over. I think she was relieved I had brought along Esther as my wing woman so she could be the poly panther goddess she was. While she was always loyal, sometimes I could tell that she felt restrained by the duty of it, wishing she was free to roam without being responsible for my or anyone else's experience.

Esther and I looked at each other, totally out of our depth, and walked over to the bar to get a drink. We stood in a corner for a while, sipping on our vodka sodas and watching the movements in the main room. The air was so salty and sticky with desire, you could almost see a faint peach haze of lust. There were all kinds of bodies, and all kind of human configurations. Twos, threes, fours, fives. I had to stop my jaw dropping to the ground. I had never seen anything like this.

As we sipped our drinks in silence, a couple approached us and asked if it was our first time here. Clearly, it was obvious. Esther got into a nice conversation with them, and I think I ended up dissociating a little, zoned out by too much stimulus and perhaps knowing I didn't really want to be there. I woke from my state to Esther tapping my shoulder and whispering, "Hey I think I want to change wrist band colors. I am kind of curious, and I want to go with these guys and explore a bit. They said they've got a private room upstairs."

This was the last thing I had expected from Esther. I was shocked but also kind of proud of her. "Here, you take mine.

I should have chosen red in the first place. This isn't my vibe at all."

"Are you sure?" Esther looked hesitant.

"Yes, babe. Go, go, go. I'm going to wait here, but I want you to come back in a little while and let me know if you're feeling safe, and then I'll likely head home. Okay?"

"Got it. Thanks, you're such a good friend, Lena. Wish me luck!" The woman in the couple took her hand and the three of them sauntered off to play.

So, there I was, sitting at a sex party alone, feeling like more of a prude than ever, deeply disappointed in myself. Just then, a French male voice spoke over my shoulder, *"Ma belle*, why so sad?" And standing to my back right was one of the most delicious looking specimens I'd ever seen. He may have even been better than the guy in my dreams. And the outfit was close enough. Black jeans and black devil horns. No shirt.

After I managed to pick my jaw up off the floor and unparalyzed my tongue, I replied, "I'm not really sure this is my scene." My voice went up at the end like it was more of a question than a statement.

"It's not for everyone, *c'est vrai*,' he said. "I'm Lucas. *Comment t'appelle tu?*"

"I'm Lena," I replied, my high school French serving me well in the moment.

That night, the gorgeous Lucas and I ended up chatting and spooning all night. Once Esther reappeared to let me know she was safe and that I could leave, he and I decided to take a walk and get some air.

As we walked in the balmy evening, we exchanged nutshell versions of our life stories, including rushed skip throughs of our childhood trauma. His mother had left when he was young, and he'd been raised by his father on the outskirts of Paris, and at age sixteen began modelling. But his real passion was sculpting. He'd been in the kink scene since age twenty-one and practiced ethical non-monogamy.

I was entranced by this specimen of a man. It was if he was out of a movie or soft-porn novel. His chiseled body, his perfect lips, his sandy brown hair that fell over his piercing green eyes. Just wow. We ended up back at my place and chatted and cuddled. No sexy business, not even one kiss. My pussy was on fire, longing for him to reach for me, but either he wasn't attracted to me or that red band on my wrist commanded far more respect than I wanted it to.

At around six am, he made a move to leave. "You're so special, Lena," he offered as he hugged me tight and brushed my hair behind my ear. "Let's hang out again soon?"

"Sure," I said. And with that, he was gone.

If men like Lucas were in the ENM scene, that was where I wanted to be. He'd told me aside from sex parties, another way to explore was through apps that were made for people exploring their sexuality. He'd indicated that loads of people (him included) needed a connection first, and that perhaps it was simply the party/orgy vibe that didn't click with me. I'd told him I'd take a look. So, with a coffee in one hand, and phone in another, I downloaded Mortex and began making my profile. ENM world, here I come!

As previously planned, the next day I met Esther and Charlie for lunch and a debrief. Charlie had some very interesting stories to tell about a threesome experience as well as a group of five men and her, and one lucky dude who she'd taken home to ride out the night with... literally.

"Aren't you sore?" asked Esther innocently.

"Never!" Charlie cackled.

"But what about you, Miss Esther?" I prodded. "How was it with that lovely couple you met? How did the night end up?"

'Well," started Esther. "They were so lovely, and she went down on me, and I went down on him and then I actually.... had sex with a woman for the first time in my life, and then him too! Oh my god, I can't believe I did that," she squealed.

"Go, Esther, that's my girl," sang Charlie.

"Wow," was all I could muster. "Are you going to see them again?"

"They've invited me for dinner on Friday." She smiled gleefully.

We spent the rest of the lunch chatting, joking and eating. But a part of me felt uncomfortable. Jealous even. I was used to Charlie's sexcapades. But how could Esther be kinkier than me? Even while thinking and feeling, I was aware how childish and petty I was being. I was happy for Esther, I really was. But... what about me?

I hadn't told the girls about Lucas. I lied and said I went home to bed. I'm not sure why I did that. But I guess it felt like a sacred experience that I didn't want Charlie to pull apart. I wanted it just for me. I had told them someone at the party had mentioned the Mortex app, and that I'd downloaded it, so we did have some fun tweaking my profile and swiping a bit. I had six matches by the time lunch was over. And so, instead of processing how I felt and my strange pangs of jealousy, I buried myself in swiping and planning a series of dates. I was going to have my ENM experience, one way or another.

A few months and a series of dates later, I swiftly concluded that the ENM scene didn't feel right for me. Even though there was a part of me that wanted to be swinging naked from chandeliers (or something like that) at sex parties, exploring threesomes or casually dating two or three men, no matter what I tried to open up to it all, my heart said, "no thank you."

When I'd meet a guy from the Mortex app, there was generally one of two experiences that would unfold. Either I would feel pressure or expectation to open my legs, which would have me contracting, shutting down and running from the experience (expectation was a huge no-no for my pussy) or I'd feel a connection, get the butterflies and want to craft the connection into something more meaningful, and ultimately, exclusive. And because the whole point of the scene I was exploring was to love freely and without commitment, it didn't work.

I'd either find myself shutting down or feeling devastated that I'd met a nice person who simply didn't want what I wanted. It became clearer and clearer that I was a monogamous kind of girl. No matter how much I pushed myself to be open, playful or experimental, that wasn't going to change. In the end, I learned to stop forcing myself to want something I didn't want.

I felt incredibly frustrated with the realization that I wasn't built for the poly scene. I'd noticed that there were so many great men (and women) who were part of it, and the inability to belong reflected my loneliness back to me. Ever curious, I'd been asking each person I dated for their take on the whole scene. I wanted to understand it better, and if I'm honest, I kept hoping that if I understood it better, I'd be able to engage with it.

I received a range of responses throughout my era of inquiry. They ranged from enjoying variety, to valuing freedom, to not wanting to repeat past traumatic relationship patterns, to having more people to love and support, rather than just one. I also listened to stories that held moments of the greatest ecstasy along with some of the most complex relational drama I had ever heard. They felt cinematic or soap opera-ish. All consuming. Highs and lows. Life or death. And so much processing to hold it all.

One man got honest and raw in a moment of post-orgasm intimacy and revealed, "To let one person hold your whole heart is just too terrifying to even consider. For me, being poly is a protective process." His words struck a deep chord in me. I thought back to my realization about being emotionally unavailable. Love was fucking terrifying. Partnership was a huge risk. But I wanted it more than anything in the world.

In the end, my peek into the poly world showed me that we are all looking for a next-level kind of love, something better than what we've been conditioned to believe is possible. Something uplifting, freeing and nourishing. And what that love looks like is completely up to the individual, couple or group. There is no such thing as one size fits all love.

Validation

Let this be your

Sanctuary

The place where it is

Safe to rest

Where love isn't dependent

On your hustle

Brilliance or acclaim

Where you are celebrated

Simply for your breath

Your inherent nature.

For a time

This may seem strange

Your skin prickling with

Discomfort or disbelief

And the voices you carry

May get louder

Trying to trick or

Shame you

Into movement

Stories

Of productivity and purpose.

But as you keep

Catching yourself

Returning to the sanctuary

The nest that you

Lovingly weaved

With all your healing work

You'll let the stories

Be stories

That are no longer yours.

Blinking your eyes

As a new world

Materializes around you

Where you breathe more fully

Sleep more deeply

Dance with abandon

And no longer question your

Validity.

You are valid

Without those stories

Prizes or reflections

Of a world

That is waiting

For your fucking exhaustion.

You are valid in your rest

You are valid in your peace

You are valid.

All my life, I'd been taught to perform for love. To get the grades for a pat on the head. Be a good girl to get a treat. Wear the short skirt to get the guy's eyes on my prize. Give to receive. Earn my own money, so I don't show any need. Get into the gym and prove this old mama is MILF quality and not some old maid who'll go unseen. And the return on investment for all this performance, was meant to be love… but really it was anything but.

So many of us are seeking validation, not love. And then when we get empty verbal or societal reflections or feedback, we wonder why we are emptier than before. Because we have been going about it all the wrong way.

After forty plus years of validation seeking behavior, I was hungrier than ever for love. To be honest, I was feeling quite crazy about it all. What was wrong with me? I was a successful, attractive, fit, compassionate and giving woman with great boundaries. I was a catch (if I did say so myself). And I was sick of getting the question on a first date "So, why are you still single?" Sometimes, I'd imagine my head spinning round on my neck and steam coming out my ears and yelling in a weirdly deep monster voice, "Because all you men are fucking useless. Shut your stupid mouth!" But instead, I'd smile sweetly and say, "Um, I'm just waiting to meet the right guy for me," and bat my mascaraed eyelashes and pout my mouth a little. Just enough to say, "Come get me, big boy. Are you my guy?"

No one had come close to being my guy in years. And therefore, I hadn't come close to being anyone's girl in years. It was all quite scary.

I had processed the whole seeking validation bit, but something wasn't working. Every time I went to a restaurant, sat at the beach or even walked the supermarket aisles, there were couples everywhere. And mainly average, nothing remarkable to report, kind of people. Who were partnered. Coupled up. In love. Loving each other well.

Why was it so hard for me?

"Your expectations and focus are all wrong," said Naomi. We were sitting down to Mexican and Margheritas in Sydney's inner west. I was visiting Sydney, and we'd spent the day shopping for her wedding dress. I'd been careful to zip my mouth with all my lovesick bullshit and focus on her. But Nai being Nai, once we sat down to dinner after five hours of dress fittings and gushing, she turned the spotlight on me. "You've been a great friend all day, Lena," she said. "But it's like I can hear your heart talking. You're wondering when it's going to be your turn to look at dresses, aren't you?"

I was a little taken aback. I wasn't gunning for a walk down the aisle, but I was dreaming about coupling up, making a home with someone, nesting. And if a wedding was on the cards,

I'd be open to that too. It was crazy how Nai could see right through me sometimes.

"I wanted today to be all about you, Nai. We don't have to talk about my lonely heart today."

"Don't be silly, Lena. I'm not some bridezilla, you know that."

I did know that. Big plump tears fell silently from my eyes into my fish tacos. I took a sip of my spicy marg to calm myself. "What do you mean my expectations and focus are all wrong?" I asked. "Are you saying I need to lower my expectations?"

"Lower, no. Adjust, yes," she clarified. "It's like you're looking for some perfect guy on paper and not giving them a chance to show you who they are. And on the flipside, you're trying to present as the perfect woman, and not giving them a chance to see who you are, which is a beautiful, loving woman. Love isn't about job titles, or money, or how fit you are. Look at me, I have a thousand wobbly bits and a slightly above average salary. And my fiancé is a tall, skinny, kind of dorky-sweet guy, but we are deliriously happy. There's something going on about validating the wrong kinds of things. Getting lost in the checklist. The façade. Love's never going to be there."

I was a little bit stumped. I knew there was truth in what she was saying. And of course, I wanted real deal love, not some false version of it that was based on some kind of warped validation system. "I don't know who I am without my bells and whistles. And I like shiny things," I pouted. I didn't know whether to laugh or cry.

"I've got two challenges for you to make a start," she replied. "First, take your career off your dating profile. And don't reject a potential match based on his career either."

I squirmed in my seat. "Ok, and what's the second one?" I asked.

"Try some low-key dates. Active wear or shorts. No fabulous dresses. Fish and chips, no Michelin stars. See what happens when you take the performance out of it."

"I can do that," I said sheepishly.

"The real you is an epic masterpiece, babe," she validated.

A part of me questioned this loving statement, but I simply took a swig of my cocktail and changed the topic back to all things wedding.

Later that night, back at my Airbnb, I ran a bath with Epsom salts, essential oils and rose buds. I lit a candle and brewed some chamomile tea. Sacred healing baths were a big part of my self-care routine. They always brought me home to myself without question. I did a breath meditation and set some intentions to show up for love, without the bells and whistles, without needing to work for it. Without icing myself into the most fabulous cake in the patisserie.

As I did, a little voice inside me said, "What if no one will love you like that?" My scared invalidated inner child felt so vulnerable here in the bathtub with me. "You are so lovable. You don't even need to try," I told her. Huge cries heaved up from my core, into my chest and into the warm scented air of the bathroom. Intuitively, I wrapped my arms around myself and stroked my arms.

"You are made of love," I told myself over and over.

Santa Monica Mermaid

She sat among

The spinning world

People all around her

Lonelier than ever

Wondering why

She was flapping her wings

Solar power

For thankless fireflies.

She caught herself

Holding her breath

Suspended

Waiting for something to happen

For someone to come

But it was always the same.

The odd smile

Some strange baring of teeth

A little nod

A living painting

A portrait

Of a half-life.

So she unbuttoned her dress

Walked naked

Down the pier

And dove into

The endless ocean

Home to her merfolk.

A few months later, I was sitting having a spicy margarita, sashimi and oysters at an Osteria at Santa Monica beach watching the sunset. I had just finished a three-week teaching tour in New York, Austin and L.A. I was emotionally exhausted, but at the same time, feeling enlivened and hopeful about the future of humanity. I could feel the world was hungry for healing, that change was happening.

When I taught, I co-created an incredibly subtle space with the participants. A field of consciousness, compassion, intention, reverence. It was truly beautiful to weave and relate in it together. Heartwarming, playful, the most peaceful revolution. And as was often the case, when I exited the temporary matrix we created together, the outside world felt stark, abrasive, maladapted and disconnected. It felt lonely here.

I'd promised myself not to date on this trip. Usually, when I flew around the world for work, I'd swipe a little in each city and arrange a date or two or three, depending on how long I was there. Sometimes I'd have an incredible experience, but more often than not, I would be met with an unconsidered lug of a man I couldn't connect to at all. And it would make this feeling of disconnection bigger and sometimes trigger a profound sense of grief and aloneness.

So, on this trip, I decided to sit with and metabolize that sense of loneliness that came with being a global trailblazer, rather than hide from it in the below average international dating scene. As I said yes to sitting with myself, I said no to leaking my energy or entering non-resonant dynamics. I also said yes to orienting to something greater. My hope surrounded my grief like a warm cocoon. I felt like a mermaid caught between land and sea. Feet or fins. I had spent so much time walking the earth, working, it felt like time to return to the ocean, to swim, to float, to play.

After that trip, I decided to strop travelling quite so much for work. And stop dating so widely. I decided to slow down and call in the life, the love that I really craved. Simpler. Deeper. Quieter. More creative. More playful. Less complexity. Less structure. Less agenda. My mermaid era.

Don't Hold Back

Lay it all on the table honey

Don't hold back

Your beat is strong enough

No unrequited reverie

Will crush it.

Speak your love into the balmy air.

Let it live.

Sometimes my heart would feel so full of longing that it felt like it would burst. Lust, love, loss... the longing to give and receive. It was as if there was nowhere for my longing to land. Sometimes it escaped as juicy tears of love lost or never realized. Other times the gnarling half-swallowed screams I'd allow myself in times of excessive sexual and romantic frustration. Or sometimes I channeled my longing into whopping self-pleasure orgasm sessions. And on the odd occasion, I'd get really fucking itchy and go find some boring boy to bonk for a bit. Just to let a bit of dirty water out the bathtub of my desire.

Like many of us, I'd been taught to pack my longing away. Fold it up into a neat little pocket square and hide it inside my heart. I'd been taught to hold back my desire and walk through the world with a poised pace, and a pretty, manicured façade. This wasn't just in love, but in life too. Stay in your lane. Keep quiet. Wait your turn. Good things come to those who wait. Don't jump the queue. Play by the rules.

Those fucking rules again. Conditioned to believe that if I stayed quiet and waited like a 'good girl', everything would come to me. All in good time. And when it came to love, I'd learned 'don't wear your heart on your sleeve'. Keep cool. Don't show all your cards. Don't be too much. Too needy. Too demanding. Basically, I learned, "Shut the fuck up, Lena. Don't you dare live your life from the heart."

And for years, I had listened. To my dad. My mum. My siblings. The powers that be that shape this loveless world we live in. All those dreadful Instagram dating 'experts' that tell you how to get the guy or the girl. The rules of love. I even listened to my girlfriends who kept telling me how to behave.

And one day it just felt like I was choking on my own longing. On this particular day, I was longing for Lucas. Since we had met at the sex party, we had been building a friendship. A 'share your deepest soul's desires and spoon all night' friendship. There had been no sex, nudity or even a kiss. Lots of eye gazing, arm stroking and snuggling up. I couldn't tell if he was my lover in waiting or a best friend I needed better boundaries with. But my heart was bursting for this man. I thought of him multiple times a day, and he began to be the one I naturally gravitated towards to share about my day, reach for when I was down, or call to celebrate. I just wanted him.

"But what if he doesn't feel the same way?" I asked Tabitha in our session that week.

I was exploring the idea of telling him how I felt. That I wanted to take our relationship to the next level. I wanted to be his girlfriend. Or at least one of them. I had decided ENM wasn't for me. But this was his lifestyle choice, and I wanted to be part of his romantic world. So much that it had me questioning my own preferences.

"But what if he does, Lena?" Tabitha challenged. "It seems like you're so set on protecting yourself from heartbreak that you're also blocking yourself from the potential of love."

"I don't know if I can handle the rejection or the loss of what we have. It's just so special," I mused.

"Heartbreak is inevitable," Tabitha stated. "Whether it's tomorrow, next week, next year or at death, there will always be heartbreak. It's time you stop running from what is a part of life. For all of us."

The words hit a superhighway inside my chest, and I felt my lips downturn and hot tears prick my eyes. "You're right. I am always running from heartbreak. It feels like I've had enough of it in my life, but I totally get that my self-protection is hindering me. In so many ways."

"Lean in," Tabitha said. "I'll look forward to the update next week."

As I left the treatment room and stepped into the sunshine, I took a deepened breath and gave myself a little pep talk. I needed to extend my therapy session into my own inner dialogue. "You've got this, Lena. You can take a rejection. It's not going to shatter you. How will anyone ever know what's in your heart, if you don't open it and let it speak? Let love lead."

I had no idea how Lucas would respond. But that night as we lay in arms talking about our weeks, I peered up at him with unmasked eyes full of longing and simply said, "Lucas, I want you." Clear, simple. No frills. Visceral. Felt. My breath caught for a microsecond, awaiting potential rejection.

His arm that had been laying gently around my waist gripped a little firmer, and he pulled me into him and kissed me deeply, returning that same longing without words. We didn't speak for hours. We made love passionately. Quietly. Gently.

Frenetically. In every way possible. And fell asleep in our messy sweaty sex nest.

The next morning, I woke to feel his beautiful body behind mine, a soft spoon. His breath rising and falling, echoing in my ears. A thousand thoughts and feelings rushed through me and stressed-out butterflies circled my stomach. I had no idea what was going to happen next. And that fucking terrified me. I intertwined my fingers in his as they lay across my belly, turned my head back towards him and gently kissed his tanned cheek, morning breath and all. "Good morning," I whispered.

Before we can even fathom to love and be loved, we need to decondition from all the ways we have been taught love must exist. In the end, it has no structure, form or rules... it simply is.

Part 2 Soveriegn

Lips Of Freedom

I can smell oppression

A mile away

Even when it masquerades

As love.

The ingenuity

The words that lure

The promises

Never to be fulfilled

The unspoken hooks

The offerings

Laced with chains.

The problem is

Oppression

Appears to be everywhere

It's become so normal

That the oppressors

Don't even know

They are doing it.

So everyone nods

And smiles

But behind our eyes

The light dims

And the voices

Inside our heads

Tell us

Something doesn't feel right

But we don't speak it.

Darling, let me speak it for you.

So your lips

May learn

To demand

Your freedom.

Merci, By body

My body knew

All along

That you were not

The right man for me.

The clench of my heart

The fire in my belly

The anxious prickles

That taunted my skin.

They visited me

Every single time.

I became so used to

Self-pathology

In this foolish age

Of Instagram therapy

And demi-gods.

"You are the problem"

Yelled the gaslighting voices

Of the metaverse

And the remnants of

My mangled parents

In the crevices of my head.

And so, I ignored

My brave body.

I even turned

My tears

And the welts

On my porcelain skin

Into my own

Dysfunction.

And the more

Of a fuck up

I became in the story

The higher

Your pedestal grew

And the prettier

My projection of you

Became.

I kept walking into

Storybooks

Where I was

The hysterical white girl

Privileged problems

No right to my pain.

"This is not the Holocaust.

So

Shut

Your

Mouth."

But one day

I woke up

And decided

To stop

Listening to your shit

And to let my body

Speak to me.

It told me

This is not your pain

You keep searching

For those men

Who are aching

Under the weight

Of their own torture.

No capacity

To love

To hold

To care

Even if they want to.

Just

Like

Your

Mother.

Fuck.

I had fought so hard

To disentangle myself

From the web

Of her pain

And I guess

A little piece

Of my unconscious

Really couldn't make sense

Of the world

Without her.

Existential enmeshment.

My body showed me

The hole in my heart

That I'd kept finding a way

To plug

With the wounded men

Of the world.

I peered into

The void

Whispered words

Of love

Into the place

From which I had sprung

Filled it with

Rose petals

And sealed it

With the finest beeswax.

An alter inside my chest

To pray to

Each day

Waving my sage feather

And laying crystals

On the graveyard

Of my heart.

Merci, merci, merci

My body.

Thank you for letting me listen.

Merci encore.

My body was always warning me about men who were no good for me. It's just, I didn't know how to listen.

Fourteen years earlier....

Life had just started to get good. I had come off the back of four years of hell. Totally split apart by a mental health crisis. A triple cocktail of meds that had fragmented my psyche so badly. Living in a converted janitor's closet. Smoking a pack a day. Engaging in all kinds of risky behavior. Sex, drugs and rock and roll without the glamour, but all the grit. It was survival time. Credit card debt up to my eyeballs. Living on Coca-Cola, rice and the occasional splurge for some fries. Once a month, my mother would drop off some groceries and look me in the eyes full of pity and say, "I'm so sad for you." Then she'd be gone again. Thanks, Mum.

Love came with pity. With shame. With food and toiletries.

I was so dissociated and so fucking crazy during those years. And spinning in my web of chaos and trauma. It's no wonder that when I leaned into a relationship with my now ex-husband Joseph, it was seeded in survival rather than love. And it's no wonder that we both confused the two.

Back then, my consciousness was nowhere near as developed as it is now. So, I had no idea anything was wrong with our relationship. But I knew something was wrong with my life. That the meds the sleezy psychiatrist was leaving for me at reception each month were making it worse. That I needed to get a better place to live. A better job. So, as is my way, I made these things happen. I detoxed off the meds. Wrote a resume. Got a good job. Paid the deposit on an apartment. And I brought Joseph with me. Wrote his resume.

Coached him for his interviews. And suddenly, there we were in a newly built apartment, a double income couple, winning at life.

Not long after we reached this 'next level' in the real time video game we were living in, Joseph proposed. It was the natural next step. And because I had been conditioned to believe this was exactly what I should want, and because we had done well clinging to each other and making some headway in the existential nightmare of life, there was enough evidence to lead me to believe that this was the right choice. That he was the right man for me. That all my Christmases had come at once.

My body told me a different story.

Shortly after the proposal, I fell ill. It started with gut issues.

Gut feelings that go unheard or ignored have a habit of spreading to illness, in one way or another.

After my gut shut down, the illness spread to my legs, resulting in severe bruising, nerve damage and paralysis. The doctors couldn't diagnose what was happening to me. It remained a physical mystery that came along with some up and down mental health symptoms. But no one, including me, looked at the relational dynamic or systemic implications of what was happening to me.

I became a sick woman who was lucky to have a fiancé who would put up with my fatigue, diet restrictions, lack of sexual appetite and immobility. I became a woman who was lucky to have someone help her fill her weekly pill box with dozens of pills. I was lucky he didn't leave me. By the wedding a year later, I was puffed up on autoimmune drugs, popping oxy every four hours, and counting my blessings that there was someone there to care for me through what was the beginning of an eleven-year-long nightmare.

There was care. There was commitment. There was support. But there was also shame. Blame. The removal of financial agency. The pressure to lay down, open my legs and take it, even when I didn't want to. The silent punishment of withdrawal that followed attempted boundaries. And through the marriage, I became more and more powerless. More and more dependent. Less and less expressed. I also became more and more demanding. More and more particular. More and more resentful. A shitshow where two hearts were trying hard but tearing each other apart in the most diffuse and unspeakable ways hidden underneath the image that we projected to the world of the most loving couple ever.

I don't want to say my relationship made me sick, because it's far more complicated than that. But I do believe my body was speaking to me, telling me something wasn't relationally right for years. My inability to decipher the somatic language of my body caused it to spiral. And the medical and social systems that received me and sought to support me were also, in many ways, deaf or blind, unable to understand the systemic nature of my distress and disease.

The year before Joseph and I divorced was the year I started to reconnect to my agency. The year I detoxed off the meds that were keeping me dissociated. The year I started to set some boundaries around my body. The year I found my voice. While I had no security in the world, my sovereignty became my top priority. As I claimed this bit by bit, my body stopped screaming at me. I found my health. But this healthy version of me was not a fit for the partnership I had entered as a survival-fueled young woman simply trying to survive, simply trying to feel safe.

As I began to listen to my body, and decipher its signals, I learned that what I had thought was safety was actually some kind of fancy prison. While the world beyond it seemed incredibly scary, I knew that if I were to stay well in this lifetime, I needed to walk into the fresh air. And so, I did. Totally insecure, yet totally sovereign.

I left.

My body breathed a sigh of relief, but it was only for a second. It was a bit like prisoners who have been in jail for so long that when they are released, they feel totally overwhelmed by their freedom and have a desire to go back in their cell. It takes time to acclimate. Time to learn how to walk through the world with the kind of accountability that freedom demands.

I didn't give myself that time. Instead, I buried myself deep into another relationship, one that was far more acute and insidious than the slow corrosive burn of my marriage. This is not an uncommon move after divorce, I have learned.

The fear of being alone and doing the deep healing and practical life work to find both sovereignty and security is too confronting. So, we tend to hide in any relationship we can find. The intensity. The drama. The chaos. It can all feel far more comfortable than our own healing.

So when I met Harley, the Chinese American business mastermind, I did exactly that, I buried myself in him. In us. He was very quick to destroy me. And again, my body was very quick to let me know something wasn't right. This time, instead of over a decade, it took me a little less than a year to listen, decipher and respond to my beautiful body… and to leave.

Squid Ink

You squirmed

When I shone

My psychological

Torch

Over your holes.

The poor potholes

Where your spirit

Had eroded

So long ago.

But then you

Softened.

Compassion does that.

The absence of

Judgement

To be seen in our

Imperfection

Can be the most

Healing thing

Yet also the most dangerous.

Swaying between

Two doors

Healing or hate.

As you bathed under

The light of my

Seeing eyes

I think the little

Lost boy

Inside you

Thought he'd found

Salvation

Or perhaps some kind of

Sick permission

To unleash

The load you'd been

Carrying

On me.

Making it my job

To heal and love you

No matter what.

And so, for a second

I disappeared

And became

The mother you never had

The therapist you

Desperately need

Anything but an

Equal participant

In our dance.

Such a familiar place.

I'm unsure if it's a

Pedestal

Or a dungeon

It's hellish either way

So I spoke up

Pushed back

Called you

As kindly as I could

To be the man I deserved.

But you couldn't.

The door to healing

Vanished

So, you opened the other

And hate started

Seeping out

Like squid ink

Between your teeth

And my nervous system

Fired with fear

And all the imprints

Of those men whose

Lair I'd been lured to before.

This time

Instead of freezing

Or appeasing

I told you to leave.

Perturbed

Protected

Proud

Reminding myself

I will NEVER

Be locked

In any man's dungeon

Ever again.

When we put each other on pedestals, there's always going to be some kind of power game that ensues. When we fill the holes in each other with liquid love, in an unconscious attempt to bind us together, there's always going to be a sticky mess. Cats stuck up in high tree branches. Flies caught in honey.

Harley tuned me into a crazy cat of a woman, my tail permanently frizzy from distress. His honey-laced words lured me into his harmful hands. Giving up my power, my agency again in the search for love. Over the course of a year, I transitioned from a disconnected marriage into a toxic trauma bond. Harley was a poisonous lily pad in the pond of my progress.

During that year, I met Harley at a business networking event in Singapore. He was a tall, slender and unassuming man. He looked like a cross between a musician and an academic. His sleek black Asian hair pulled into a low bun, a cool goatee, his

Chinese collared shirt, loose white pants and the notebook he carried with him everywhere he went. There was a quiet power to him. His eyes were curious, and his mind was always processing. He seemed wise; quietly powerful.

In the year leading up to my divorce, I had opened my own therapy clinic. I was making my mark in the Singapore healthcare scene and had started attending networking events to meet people and continue building connections and referral pathways. Harley was a healthcare business investor. And he had his eye on me. Professionally, at first. But it soon became personal. Very personal.

I'd been speaking with a bunch of medical doctors about the link between anxiety and trauma and he quietly joined the group, staring down at me, watching as I commanded the attention and respect of the group. After the conversation ended and everyone dispersed, he spoke.

"You're very impressive, Lena. I've been following your journey here in Singapore. You're onto something. And you have very attractive energy."

In that moment, he hooked into my deep-seated need for validation from men and authority. He represented both. Although I didn't know it at the time, I was instantly in the early stages of trauma bonding with him. A slow sizzle emerged in my belly, and I smiled like a cat who had been fed the best quality cream. Warning signals masquerading as chemistry. Professional flattery firing up my deep-seated daddy issues.

"Thank you," I replied. "I'm interested to know more about your work in healthcare here and see if there's a potential to collaborate."

Harley was a prominent figure in the Singapore healthcare sector, and everyone knew that he held a lot of power and the kind of capital that could move mountains. His name often came up in my professional circles, and while I'd seen him at events before, I'd never dared approach him. He was playing in another league altogether.

My business hat was on. Little did I know, that just as he was manipulating me, I was also tapping into his core wounding around being unworthy, useless and disposable. Harley had come from a family system where the mother was the tyrant who he needed to serve, and his father was the useless larrikin who was never enough for his wife. So, somewhere in his psyche, he had a lot to prove; the narrative of the useless man who is desperate to be deemed worthy mingled up with an undercurrent of hatred for the alpha female which in this case was me.

I had no idea that our inner children were already playing a poisonous game of ring-a-rosies.

We arranged to have lunch the following week to explore business opportunities. At the lunch, he continued to flatter me, the progress I had made, my knowledge of trauma, my ability to speak to 'elders' and open doors.

"I can help you," he offered. "There's only so far a white woman can go in Asia alone. To have the support of a respected Chinese healthcare investor will take you to new heights. You are a star. You just need the right help to shine."

"Yes, exactly!" The little girl inside me who was desperate to be seen and supported beamed. Manipulation successful.

We continued meeting to explore potential ways to work together. Always over a meal. There was something very anthropological about eating together. He liked taking me to new places, ordering for me, serving me. And it very quickly went from purely business to a social engagement.

Just as his unconscious tentacles were out, so were mine. I began to ask him more personal questions. I always had a knack for seeing people behind the façade they presented to the world, and at first it would disarm them, but then it would endear me to them, particularly if they had the trauma of being unseen, which so many men do.

So as he continued to flatter me and feed me, I continued to make him feel seen, useful and powerful. Our encounters became the highlight of my week. I felt connected, valued and wanted. None of it was romantic. The romance (if you can even call it that) only began once I had signed away my authority, given him agency over my business, my name, my money. It became some kind of reward or, rather, punishment. Something he could use to keep me trapped in his grip.

Harley convinced me to sign away half of my business to him. His promise was to bring me more clients, raise my authority in Asia and build an unstoppable clinical business together. He seduced me with talk of money, fame and a lifelong partnership. From the beginning, something felt wrong. His conditions felt unfair, and when I would voice them, he would retract, tell me I was being ungrateful and suggest that maybe we couldn't continue working together, eating together, connecting at all. And that I was bound for failure.

I was so deep in the trauma bond, I couldn't fathom not having him in my life. Between meetings I'd be thinking about him, daydreaming, making up futures in my head where we were business partners, lovers and this incredible interracial crusader couple changing the world. I started being unable to sleep, eat, exercise or focus. My nervous system was hijacked - in constant flight mode, desperate for our next meeting, text or email interaction. My body was talking to me, and although I had learned the lesson to listen with my ex, it seemed as though I'd forgotten it again.

There was a month of intense push and pull process, where he'd propose certain business conditions, I'd counter them, he'd shame me and pull away, and then I'd come back to the process. We were both hungry for it to happen. In the end, it was me who gave away far more than I should have to keep the connection, form the partnership. And one day, it was done. I was in a business arrangement with a man who didn't truly respect me and was pulling the strings. I became his puppet, and he, my master.

Once I had given up my business and financial power, I was primed to open my legs for him too.

We had started having dinner three or four nights a week. Our conversations got more personal. And as we got closer, my marriage got more and more rocky.

Two months later, on a particularly awful New Year's Eve, Joseph and I called it quits. And Harley was the first person I called. He came rushing over and held me while I wept.

"Don't worry, Lena. I'll take care of you. I'll help you with your visa, you can stay at my house, whatever you need. I'm here for you."

I felt at once terrified but safe. It was almost like I was in some nightmare of a movie, and he was the prince coming to save me.

A few weeks later, in the murky haze of separation, I moved into his home. It was an eerie and cold space. No art on the walls, no cushions or throws. Just some shoddy furniture, a few pots and pans and piles of paperwork all over the place. The place gave me the creeps, but I was grateful to have a roof over my head. He set me up in the spare room. I emptied my suitcase into the second-hand wardrobe and put my own sheets on the bed so it would feel a little more familiar. I brought my own pillow with me too. It was only meant to be temporary, while I was sorting out my visa, looking for an affordable place to live, figuring out how to be a single expat woman in Singapore. No easy task.

We continued eating dinner together a few nights a week. And sometimes we would go for a walk at the beach after dinner before heading home. One night, we sat on the pier at East Coast Park, and he took my hand. "Do you feel that, Lena?" he asked. "Electricity."

I did. My nervous system had been on fire since I first met this man, trying to warn me to run far, far away. The opposite of chemistry. He was fucking dangerous. And somehow, I had pegged him as a knight in shining armor, rather than the villain he was turning out to be in my story.

I nodded my head. He leant in and kissed me. And for a moment, I thought I had died and gone to heaven. Everything I had dreamed of was happening... if you closed one eye and squinted and forgot that I was going through a divorce, forgot I'd given up control of my business, forgot that I now needed a visa to stay in Singapore with my kids and my company, forgot that I was living in a weird serial killer-ish house. With a kiss, everything seemed perfect. The delusions of the traumatized little girl inside me eclipsed all else.

"I'm going to take you home to bed. We will shower first," he commanded.

I was excited by his clarity and at the idea of a shower scene. I hadn't been naked with a man in a long time. Even when I'd been having sex with Joseph, I kept my nighty on in recent years. I was excited but scared. The shower was not what I expected. He told me to wait and watch while he showered and then beckoned for me to join him. I shyly took off my clothes and stepped into the small cubicle.

I expected him to take me in his arms, but instead, he turned off the water, lathered soap in his hands, picked up a loofah and began to scrub me down. Like a dirty little girl who had been playing in the mud when she shouldn't have been. I was so shocked that I had already entered a freeze state. The me now would have been out of there. To be honest, me now would not have gotten anywhere near this creep to begin with. But back then, I was frozen, a traumatized girl in a woman's body, unable to speak, say no or leave. So, I let him scrub me down.

"You need to be clean to lie in my bed. You're a dirty *Ang-mo*," he chided. *Ang-mo*, the Chinese slang for 'white person'. When he had finished scrubbing, he took the shower hose off the wall and proceeded to spray me down. "Now clean your teeth and get into bed."

I did as I was told, and after brushing my teeth well, so he wouldn't question their cleanliness, I lay down next to him. He rolled on top of me, kissed my cheeks and my breasts, but not my mouth, put a condom on (thank goodness for that) and pumped his way to orgasm. The whole thing took about seven minutes.

I was frozen throughout.

"Now you can cuddle me while I fall asleep." He opened his arm out, and I rolled towards him and put my head on his chest. Both our nervous systems were incredibly dysregulated. I could feel the twitching inside his body and his angry blood rushing through his veins. I could feel my own nervous system sending scared prickles through my skin. My heartbeat became so loud, catching itself between beats, delayed. But it all felt familiar and, in some sick, twisted way, nice. I slept on and off that night, confused about what was happening.

The fucked up dynamic continued.

We worked together. Ate together. Sometimes he would bring me to his room to repeat a similar sexual experience. Other times he would tell me to sleep in the spare room. The ordering away often came with some kind of deprecating comment. You smell. Your tummy is too fat. I am not attracted to you. And I proceeded to feel smaller and smaller and smaller.

He started ordering me to work longer hours as a therapist. Do marketing work at night. On the weekends. He told me I needed to pay my way into the partnership. That he'd help me get a visa, so I didn't need to leave the country. That I should be grateful. Over the course of a few months, I lost myself completely. However, on the outside, it appeared that I was thriving. That we were a healthcare power couple. That everything was coming up roses.

It was at night in the solitude of my room, exhausted from working like a dog, devastated from being shunned and told how unattractive I was that the tears flowed, and my nervous system fired. This went on for months. Somewhere in the process, I had begun to alienate myself from my friends. He didn't like my friends. He'd convinced me that they were fake, a distraction from my professional and spiritual pursuits. My whole world revolved around him.

About six months in, Harley had gone on a trip to Malaysia with his family, and I arranged to have coffee with Naomi. She was visiting Singapore on a work trip. She could see my brokenness immediately. Right through my smile. Right through the bullshit I was spinning about how well everything was going.

"Babe, this isn't who you are. Be honest with me. You look awful. Exhausted. The stress is oozing out of you. You haven't been returning my calls. Spill. It's me. You're safe here."

I erupted into a fit of tears and the whole story came out.

"Fuck, Lena. This is bad. He sounds like a total narcissist. You need to get out."

"But what if he's my soul mate and I'm meant to go through all this from a spiritual perspective?" As the words came out of my mouth, I could hear my own delusion. They sounded different in the reverberations of the air than they did swirling around my tortured head.

"Listen to me. You are being abused. On every level. Emotional. Physical. Financial. You need to get out now. I'm here for you. You can call me anytime. You can even get on a plane and come and stay with me in Sydney. But you need to get out. Promise me."

"I promise," I replied. "But give me time. There's so much tied up here. My business. My money. My visa."

Something about this conversation sobered me up from the trance I had been in. I really had lost myself. It was time to free myself and find my way back to the independent, powerful woman I knew I was deep down.

It was not an easy process. Thankfully, I had Naomi on the other end of the phone and weekly sessions with Tabitha to remind me when I was losing my grip on reality, being manipulated, or losing my sovereignty. I also had the promise I made to myself. To get out, at all costs. And when I make a promise to myself like that, I always keep it.

The exit process took about six months. First, I tried to set boundaries. Asking him to lower his voice, stop calling me names. To stop ordering me around. But these attempts resulted in Harley escalating, yelling, threatening and punishing me. He started using sex and cuddles as weapons. He would offer them when I was feeling resistant or down, and take them away when I was feeling balanced or inhabited even a sniff of power.

The next thing was to stop sleeping with him and get back to business only. He'd been periodically telling me he was done with me romantically anyway, so the next time he 'dumped' me, I accepted it, instead of crying and begging him to take me back, like I'd used to. That part wasn't hard. I soon moved into a small apartment and having my own space seemed to give me a better sense of physical sovereignty. Room to self-care. To think. To plan.

However, when I told him I wanted out of the business partnership, he flipped a lid. His dark almond eyes became more oblique and angrier than usual. Hot air pushed through his nostrils, and he raised his voice to new decibels. "How dare you even think you can exit this business? I made you. You are nothing without me and I will make sure everyone in this country knows it. You will have no clients. No money. No visa. You will not survive a second. I made you!"

My whole body was shaking, my heart was beating in my chest and my throat felt like it was swelling up. I wanted to give in. To make it stop. To get back in his bed and lay on his chest. But I did none of those things. "Okay, Harley," I said quietly. "Do your worst."

Then I turned and walked out.

That evening, every communication app I had begun firing with his rage. WhatsApp. IMessage. Instagram. Facebook. Telegram. Email. Threats upon threats. Messages. Voicemails. They didn't stop. He threatened to report me to the government, revoke my visa (that was lodged under his company), not to pay me any wages. To tell all my clients I was evil. The threats were interwoven with shaming/blaming statements. Name calling. You name it. It was as if his monster that had been so well disguised had reared its ugly head and was going wild.

That night I lay on the floor in my apartment shaking, sobbing. Terrified about what was going to happen next. Naomi stayed on the phone with me for hours. I also got up the courage to call my ex and let him know what was happening. There was a chance I would have to leave the country and not be able to continue 50/50 parenting. To his credit, Joseph, who had been wary of Harley and our business partnership from the beginning, listened and offered to keep a record of all the threatening communications. Things were still very tender between us. We were co-parenting, but the rest wasn't yet sorted out. The money. The legalities. And I could tell a part of him wanted to help, but a part of him was still angry and hurting about how our marriage ended. He did let me know, that even if I had to leave the country, he'd make sure the kids would be able to see me. But he offered no support to help me navigate the situation. I suppose, when I left him, he had quite rightly decided I was no longer his responsibility.

As directed by both Naomi and Tabitha, I stopped replying to Harley's threatening messages. For a while, they got worse. More frequent. More abusive. But then they slowed down. Finally, a calmer message arrived: *Lena, we need to talk. You can't avoid me forever.*

He was right. I agreed to a zoom meeting under the condition that I could record it. He agreed.

By the time we got to the call, he must have realized that he wasn't going to lure me back in. He must have also realized that if he publicly ruined me, the story would come back to ruin his reputation. And there was nothing more important to him than that. He was very well respected in the Singapore healthcare community. It was probably the only thing he had going for him.

He arrived to the call with a clear proposal. He'd let me leave quietly. Give me time to rebrand, take my PA with me. And he'd even keep my visa current until I could find a way to get my own (which would not be easy). He had two conditions. 1) I never breathed a bad word about him and 2) I had to pay him a few thousand dollars every month as fee for his time and effort in keeping my visa. Blackmail. Pure and simple.

I agreed. Without the visa, I'd have to leave the country in 30 days. Without my children. Without an income. With nothing other than my few possessions and a few thousand dollars in the bank. It wasn't a viable option.

So I paid him off. For six months. I launched a new company. Came up with a cool rebrand story. Smiled. Didn't even blink. Once he was getting the money from me, he backed off. It took me that time to get a new visa. The Singapore government rejected my application three times. And during that time, my anxiety was at an all-time high. I had to make peace with the idea that I might be separated from my children and need to start all over again. Just as I had come to terms with the devastating possibility, I received a call from my immigration agent that my recent visa appeal had been accepted.

And just like that, I was free. Finally sovereign. Harley had no more power over me.

That night, as I sat in my little apartment with a glass of rosé, I cried and cried and cried. It was over. I could finally breathe. As I gulped the air and choked on my tears, I found myself rocking back and forth, arms around me and the words escaped my mouth, "I want my mummy."

In that moment, I realized that this deep guttural feeling was what I had been running from all along. Why I ended up with Harley. Why I ended up with Joseph. The longing to be cared for.

In the months that followed, I read everything I could get my hands on around maternal attachment trauma, abuse dynamics, and spiritual bypassing. I also went deeper into somatics, engaging in several trainings. And I doubled down on therapy. The relational plane. The somatic plane. A deep rewiring was in process. I knew that it would take years. But one thing I knew for certain... I would never give my power away to a man again.

Detox

My pretty piece of peace

Was so foreign

And new to me

That I was compelled

Into your chaos

The weight of the load

You were pushing

Up the hill of your life.

You felt familiar

Like home

The labor

The distress

The mis-wired circuitry

Lighting up

The old stories

That would always

Live in the

Archaeology

Of my kingdom.

You felt

Like the sweetest air

I'd ever tasted

Human crack

And for a moment

I thought

I couldn't live

Without you.

But as my wise spirit

Guided me away

From the hellhole

You were dancing above

The deep detox began

The damaged

Lust of it all

Began to fade

And I found my form again

Free of you

Longing for you

Purging you

And integrating you

At once.

Sitting on my

Lily pad of peace

Floating for a while

Remembering

Reorienting

Relearning

That love does not look like this.

To miss one's abuser is the most curious thing. And I did.

Once the dust settled from the atrocious Harley situation, I missed him terribly. While I didn't miss the pain of it, I missed the companionship. In some ways, I missed the intensity. The drama. Once he was gone from my life, suddenly it was very quiet. No one pushing me, taunting me, teasing me, ordering me about. No one to obsess over, worry about, make sense of.

And so, the detox began.

I went through many stages. The first was fear. It felt as if I wanted him so badly, I would die without him in my life. My nervous system was in total hyper-activation, and I was climbing the walls with anxiety. I wanted to reach out, tell him I was wrong, that I would do anything to be back in business with him, back in bed with him. The frenzy of the abused little girl inside me who didn't know how to exist without my perpetrator.

But I didn't.

I set a boundary with myself. As the distress intensified and peaked, it crossed over into grief. The huge sobbing sessions ranged from "How could he do this to me?" to "How can I live without him in my life?" to "How could I have let this happen to me?" to "I'm so lonely."

And here, in my loneliness, was where I needed to sit.

So I did.

I sat with my lonely self, daily, for about a month. I'd let myself weep for an hour in the morning and an hour in the evening. Then I'd workout, do some work, force myself to eat (my appetite really was quite low), then cry myself to sleep. My pillow was permanently tearstained. I became sluggish through the grieving stage, having to summon all my inner strength to get up and go each day. I was too embarrassed to tell anyone what I was experiencing. It was totally at odds with the strong independent woman persona I continued to project into the world. The only person I spoke to with a shred of honesty during that time was Naomi. And even with her, I muted my emotions. I was so ashamed of how I was feeling.

In time, the grieving did subside. Almost without me noticing it. Somewhere within that period, the anger began to emerge. It poked it's head up from time to time, but I would push it back down. Back then, I was not comfortable with my own rage. But I knew it was there, and it felt like a little engine that propelled me to keep going. The best revenge would be to live my best life. And although I wasn't sure what that looked like, I was damn well sure going to try and figure it out.

I got to work developing my new business. I expanded in Singapore. I launched internationally. And I knew that news of my success would reach Harley. Just thinking about it made me smirk a little. Little smoke trails of anger, resentment and some kind of sick satisfaction. *Look at me now, asshole*, I'd find myself thinking from time to time.

Over time, I started thinking less about Harley, and my energy equalized. Business was going well. I was in a good rhythm with self-care and work. I'd found equilibrium again. I poked my head out of my turtle shell and socialized. I found myself laughing, enjoying my food again. I even went out dancing one night, which I hadn't done in several years. And as I shook my hips and tossed my hair on the dance floor, I knew I was ready to start dating. To embark on the journey to love beyond trauma.

The Fisherman & The Mermaid

The chapter ended

The one where

Your sweet talk

Was laced with

Honey and poison.

Where I was

A pretty fish

On your crooked

Hook.

Where you cast me

In and out

Of the dirty

Love pool.

Luring me in

With the kind of

Cheap bait

I was craving.

Worms disguised

As the finest

Caviar

Smoke and mirrors.

Then waiting

Long enough til I'd

Licked my wounds

Swimming freely.

Other fishermen

Admiring my

Shimmering skin

It's as if you could smell it.

You'd pull me close

Throw me away

Hover nearby

So I could still feel you

Missing your honey hook.

One confused

Unconscious fisherman

With a cunning

Tongue.

So cunning

You'd even

Fool yourself

On a good day.

But I knew

There was a part

Of you who could

Taste your own poison.

So you'd cover

The scent

Head buried

In a sea of fish

Drunk on their

Perfume.

I started to

Recognize

The taste

Of your bait

Some time ago.

But I'd still

Fall for it

And shame myself

For being a

Silly little fish.

When I'd find myself

Cast back

Bleeding

In the water again.

But this time I

Saw your speak

For what it really is

All lure was lost.

As I refused to

Take your hook

I remembered....

I'm not some silly fish, asshole.

I'm a fucking mermaid

Never to be hooked again.

The unavailable man is a common species, swimming in the fucked-up dating pool. Another common species is the anxious, disempowered woman, who continues to lap up less love than she deserves. Together, they tend to do the most embarrassing unconscious dating dance. He reels her in and throws her back, again and again and again, and she swims around in an emotional turmoil, shaking her seductive ass, until she is next hooked and can start the ridiculous dance all over again.

After I recovered from my experience with Harley, I spent a good few years being one of those poor female fish. Pretty power games. Mating dances that go nowhere. A banged up old seesaw. And everyone wondering why they are still single.

After nearly two decades off the dating market, I began again in sunny Singapore. I was a fish out of water to begin with. A middle-aged, rather tall, expat woman with two kids and a growing company. It was the tail end of Covid, and in person meet cutes simply weren't an option, so the apps were my entry into the maze of middle-aged men. I had nothing to compare it to. Swipe left. Left. Left again. There wasn't much choice. Singapore is a small island. Most expat men in my age group were happily (or unhappily) married. After my experience with Harley, I decided to stay away from Chinese men. What was left was slim pickings.

But there were a few passable lads around. So, I dated. I put on dresses. Sat across the dinner table from every passable expat man I could find.

I encountered four main categories of men. The first were men my age who were recently separated or divorced and carrying an incredible amount of anger, and either it was directed to their wives or it was being projected at me. No, thank you.

The next were men in their forties or early fifties who had never been married, nor had kids. They had been chasing career growth around the globe and seemed to have an air of selfishness about them. Of this category, there were plenty who would smugly tell me that they could have three Asian women a night, if they wanted. Barf. No, thank you.

Then there were the younger group of men in their early thirties who were earlier in their career, never married, no kids and seemed to be ready for a good time, not a long time. To be fair, a few of these did want children, but more kids was not an option for me. My womb was closed for business. No, thank you.

Lastly, there were men who were married, online looking for some side action. Some of them indicated secrecy was required, while others indicated they were in an open relationship. Whether this was true or not, I'll never know. It was a hard pass for me.

So, this was the dating pool I was swimming in. Not great. But I was hungry for companionship. For touch. To even open my mouth and have someone listen to me talk about my day was an attractive offer. I was lonely. And so, I found myself working with what was available. A bunch of emotionally under-developed men who liked to talk the big talk, flash their gold cards, lean in for a few dates and then go silent, make an excuse or simply say "I'm not looking for anything serious." The classic excuse of the avoidant male.

For the first couple of years, I'd be shocked and upset when I was inevitably thrown back into the dating pool after a few dates. The magic numbers leading up to the discard tended to either be three or five. Sometimes I'd get to eight. But rarely.

Over time, something shifted inside me, and I became jaded, waiting for the discard. Guarded. A little defensive. Maybe a lot defensive. And some men would challenge me: "You've got your guard up, Lena." I'd have one of two responses. I'd either snap back, letting them know exactly why my guard was up, or I'd soften and bring it down, hoping this particular man would hold my heart.

They never did. I'd find myself back where I started. Alone again. Swiping again. Wondering what was wrong with me.

It wasn't all bad. I was having some staggeringly great sex in the process. More orgasms than I'd had at any other stage in my life. All my married friends loved living vicariously through me, hanging on for my next story, wondering what outfit I was going to wear for the next date, reports on how many orgasms I'd had that night. I was like their living real-life version of a soft porn romance novel. Dissociative, titillating entertainment. They were mostly home with their kids and disengaged husbands. Or all dressed up for a special occasion with their best underwear on, only to go to bed high and dry while their husbands watched the football or some other such offense. I could sense a little bit of jealousy when they listened to my stories. But it would vanish the moment I showed up in tears again. Dejected. Single. Alone. Their envy would be replaced with pity and the stench of superiority. Poor Lena.

I was used to the back and forth and didn't hold it against them. Their code-switching behavior mirrored my own. I'd shift from excitement and hope each time I had a good first date, to despair and resentment every time an encounter ended. It was exhausting.

The worst experiences were the ones where the men would sweet talk me into bed. Love bombing. Words of affirmation. And incredible sexual skills. Touch. My two 'love languages.' I'd go into a total gaga trance, thinking I'd found my person, and then suddenly, he'd be gone. This breed of man would have a habit of disappearing just as emotional intimacy started sparking. They'd go silent for days or weeks. And I'd go through the motions of anxiety, anger, self-blame, anguish and letting them go. It would be an intense rollercoaster of rejection.

And then just as I stopped hoping for them to message or call and begin to move on... PING! There would be a message from them, with some excuse.

"I was travelling."

"Work was insane."

"I needed space."

"I've had a lot on my plate with my kids and ex."

Whatever the excuse, it would come with some kind of compliment as well as an invitation.

"I've missed you."

"I've been thinking about you."

"You're on my mind."

"Are you free for dinner?"

"I want to come over and make you cum."

"Shall I bring some prosecco and berries to yours after work tonight?"

And little old me, desperate for some company, to have my body stroked and to feel their face buried between my legs, would often say, "Sure, see you soon."

And the cycle would repeat.

A couple of years into my 'anxious fish phase', Ellen sat me down for a stern talk. I think she'd hit her limit of listening to me cry and moan when some idiot dumped me or disappeared.

"What do you expect, Lena?'" she exclaimed. "You keep making excuses for these men. No one is too busy to message or call. You're letting them get away with such bad behavior. You keep going back for more. Making it easy for them to crawl into your bed. You need to stop dating unavailable men. And stop listening to their sob stories. Boo-hoo. Wa-wa. You need to cut them loose the moment you notice their inconsistency. Words and actions not matching. Excuses. You're better than that. I'm sorry I'm being harsh, but this really needs to stop now."

I felt my cheeks burning crimson. "You're right. I need the harshness. It's time for a shift. Okay, no more unavailable men. No more letting them coax me into bed. No more."

"Good," she affirmed. "Now go fix your crown and catch a prince, darling. You deserve so much more."

I squirmed a little at the idea of catching a prince, but I understood the intention behind her slightly mismatched words. She wanted me to hold out for a good guy that was going to treat me well. I wanted that, too, but how to make that happen, I wasn't exactly sure of. But I vowed to try.

After that conversation, I started to see more clearly when a man was spinning stories early on. I'd usually have it figured out by date two. And I'd end it. For the first time, it was me saying "No, no, thank you, no."

In the beginning, it felt good. I felt empowered. But as time went on, I remained single. Sure, I wasn't letting men manipulate me anymore. But honestly, it felt like cobwebs were growing in my knickers. And a gold chest plate was growing on top of my heart. Instead of being too 'easy', I'd developed a huge list of conditions to date me. What began as protection had turned into the armor of disconnection.

As I sat with this epiphany one evening by my pool, I wondered, "How do I do this? How do I be soft and lean in while also protecting my heart?" It all felt too hard. I felt emotionally exhausted from dating that led to nowhere, lost in the Bermuda triangle, where love can't live.

Daisy Chains

My love cost me

My freedom

My freedom cost me

My love.

It feels like

This world is

Asking me

To choose

Just one.

And no matter which

One I choose

I lose.

A crowded cage

Or any empty

Auditorium

The rides at the fair

Are not as fun

With just one.

Pink fairy floss

An empty bed

Or the weight of your

Bag of pain.

I'd rather sit

In a field

And make

Daisy chains.

Conditions become oppression.

I'd been in my fair share of oppressive relationships. And worked hard to break free from every single one of them. In most cases, my oppressors had no idea that they were asking me to give up some level of my freedom or authenticity to be loved.

I think part of the reason I remained single for so long was because at the first whiff of power play, my spirit had me running for the hills. When you've lived in oppressive dynamics for so long, freedom becomes incredibly precious, and you'll do absolutely everything to keep it. Freedom had become one of my guiding principles in life. And not just in romantic relationships. In my friendships, my family dynamics, my business. And I wanted freedom not just for me, but for everyone I related with, on every level. Freedom breeds peace and power. Yet it takes far more accountability than oppression. It comes with far more boundaries, losses, surrender and perhaps loneliness.

Because I had chosen freedom above all, so much in our oppressive world didn't sit well with me. When it came to love, there was a hell of a lot that I ended up saying no to. I'd sit on the edge of the couples and families that surrounded me, in some ways longing for the intimacy that was there, but in other ways totally repelled from the sense of burden, tension and oppression that often appeared, whether in small micro-interactions, or in bigger, more manipulative or even abusive dynamics.

Charlie was a hard 'no' when it came to oppression, too. Her exit would be at lightning speed, even quicker than mine. And Esther was in the midst of extricating herself from a marriage that bound her to be the emotional punching bag of a covert narcissist.

She was still in that stage where his tricks of the light or torturous tongue could put her swiftly back into the roles of servant, self-abandonment or enabler. We'd talk long into the night when she'd find herself here again. Being taken from, punished, gaslit. And once she'd orient back around her center, her sovereignty, she'd get back on the path to freedom that she was paving, one step at a time.

To exit dynamics that oppress us is an act of bravery. And it often comes with a shattering of the self we thought we knew and a total recalibration of the world around us. It's never just one relationship where we are oppressed. The oppression is usually lurking in our friendships, our careers, in the way we speak to ourselves, and the way we treat others.

One evening, Esther called me in tears. "He's taking everything," she sobbed. "The house, the shares, even the dog. He says everything is in his name, and I can't do anything about it. I'm the one who put the deposit down. We wouldn't even have a house to fight over if it weren't for me."

"Take a pause, Esther. Breathe. Feel your feet on the floor. Let's talk this through," I calmed her. "There is no world in which he can take everything. It's not a legal possibility."

"He said he will tell the lawyers that I cheated and then I'll get nothing," Esther stammered.

"He's fucking with your mind. He's gaslighting you. He's the one who cheated. He's already living with her. And you have a string of texts to prove it was going on for months. You're not clear right now. Whatever he's said to you has messed with your sense of reality. He simply can't do any of the things he is telling you."

Esther burst into tears on the phone. "You're right. I don't know how he gets in my head like that. I'm coming back. I'm coming back." She breathed a big sigh as she sorted her psyche out.

These calls from Esther would come about every ten days or so. Her ex would say something or do something where she would lose all power. As her friend, my job was to help her regain a sense of equilibrium and find her voice, her power once more. Having exited several oppressive relationships in the past and worked with many women as a therapist who were going through separations or divorces, I knew the non-linear mind-spiraling journey all too well.

When it was time for separation or divorce, the presence of oppression became crystal clear, and for many, the quest for freedom became a war to win. I preferred to see it as a maze with many locked doors and missing keys. There was a way to move through with wisdom and perseverance rather than the whirlwind and destruction that comes with war.

However, before that moment when oppression ends and the quest for freedom begins, it's often living inside the minute moments of our relationship for years. Silently eating away at us, diminishing our light, stopping us from living the most fulfilled, harmonic existence. And it's not just women being oppressed by men. Women are oppressing men too. All the fucking time. It's as if we trap each other into tiny existential display homes and say "Stay here. Stay small. If you want to be loved, don't move, change, grow or break the mold in any way."

I'd felt suffocated in the miniature mold of my marriage for years, and it was only when I exploded out of it that I really began to come alive. Four years on, I was becoming the most unbridled version of myself. I could see Esther at the beginning of this journey. Watching her find her voice, her power, and rediscover herself as an independent woman was a privilege.

"Esther, you're in a process of reclaiming your power. I'm here to reflect that back to you any time you need." As I hung up the phone, I felt a swell of emotion rise from my belly and a big howl came up my throat. I took a pen to journal my thoughts:

We're breaking free.

All of us.

This is the end of oppression.

The reclamation of freedom.

The path of harmony begins with discord and destruction.

The rise of divorce, the exploration of polyamory or ethical non-monogamy, the ever-single souls who were saying no to relationship.... We were all, every one of us, seeking freedom. But somehow, this freedom seemed awfully lonely. I sobbed a little more, put on some sleep playlist on Spotify and curled up for a sovereign yet lonely sleep.

The quest for freedom is part of the quest for love. So, when love eludes us, we can direct our attention to all the ways we are oppressed and start to unlock those chains. Love will always follow... eventually.

Part 3 The End of Self-abandonment

Omakase-style Love

Hungry

Craving an

Omakase-style love.

Your breadcrumbs

And bits

Don't even touch

The famine

Inside me.

In fact

They make it

Worse

Tantalizing

My lovesick

Tastebuds.

They used to

To trick me

To stand on

My hind legs

Like some

Stupid dog

Waiting to

Be fed

By a shitty

Half-assed owner.

But I've learned

To sit

To stay

To self soothe

And not run

Forward

Into your

Shadowy game

Of deprivation.

Sitting with

My own

Hunger

Making Love

To my own

Spirit.

Embracing

My own

Loneliness

And holding

My tender heart

Whispering

"I

deserve

so

much

more."

Again

And

Again

Until discipline

Becomes belief

Ravenous

But no longer

Destitute

Or destructive.

Waiting patiently

For famine to become

Feast.

I'm ready for you,

My abundant love.

Kiss Of Death

Every time

You kissed me

I disappeared

A little.

Fainter

Quieter

The colors

Of my glorious self

Muted.

I let you

Kiss me

Into some kind of

Slow soul death.

Over years

Climbing mountains

Together

Fighting battles

Building castles

Winning the war

Around us

But losing myself.

A body without

A present soul

Is a dangerous thing.

Mine spoke to me

Daily

Symptoms of

Self-exile.

Your kisses

Were laced

With love

But also with

Incredible demand

Claiming my body

And banishing

My spirit.

I was too big, bold

Beautiful and wild

For you to capture

And contain

So you kissed me

To death.

You spoke

In kind tones

To my inner

Lonely little girl

Who'd been having

An epic tantrum

Inside my ribcage

For decades

And shining blinding

Light

Through my yoni

For years.

You settled the girl

But you banished

My most sacred self.

Our living saga

Was not sustainable.

One day my soul

Spoke to me

From up above

And shortly after

Came flooding back

Into my body

Home.

As I learned

To inhabit myself

Again

My colors

Revivified

And I could see

The ropes of our

Semi-scared bond

That was killing us both.

I bowed to you

And whispered

To your soul

"There's something better

Waiting out there."

These kisses

Have been

A slow death

For us both.

The little boy

Inside you

Went crimson

With shame

And the man

You'd never fully

Stepped into

Bellowed the rage

That set your own

Distressed soul

Free.

And as we stood

Face to face

Free from the spell

That had lured us

Here

Our shared timeline

Disintegrated

And two separate paths

Emerged.

I packed you

A picnic

Gave you my favourite

Blanket

To keep you warm

In gratitude and grief

As you walked on.

I turned to the mirror

That appeared

In the puddle of

My own tears

Looking at these lips

That had been kissed

Against their will.

I slid on the most

Fabulous

Fuscia pink

Lipstick

Offered my reflection

A cheeky pout

Meeting my own gaze.

Never again

I promised.

And skipped off

In search of

New life

Ready for

A different kind

Of kiss.

When we make ourselves smaller to be loved, we will never be able to receive it.

I was so hungry for love I would shrink myself into an oven-dried miniature version of myself to receive it. I would erode my own spirit. Pack parts of myself away. To become lovable. To adapt myself into the kind of puzzle piece that would fit with a man who simply wasn't right for me. Who couldn't love all of me, no matter how hard he tried. I followed this pattern many times. Neglecting myself in favor of love. Disappearing. And as I disappeared, so did love.

The first man I disappeared with was my husband, Joseph. I was already such a hot mess when I met him that I didn't really realize. I was just grateful not to be alone anymore. Grateful to have someone to share a meal with. To cry with. To go through the ups and downs of life with. On a surface level, these things are love in action.

And he did love me. He accepted my pain, rather than rejecting it, like my mother. Like my father. What a sweet relief, what a generous gift, to sit with me in my darkest hours. And I returned the favor. I loved him in his most tortured times. But while we loved each other in the pain, the hardship and the sorrow, we did not love each other's splendor, joy and aliveness.

One morning in Singapore, I returned home from morning Qi Gong in the Botanic Gardens, and I was full of life, energy and love. It was oozing out of my cells. It was during days of my physical recovery. I was getting stronger, more mobile, active even. I was finding joy and meaning through spirituality and movement practices. I was coming alive again. And on this glorious morning, I came home beaming, gathered my two children who were both so small at the time, and turned on some music, so we could dance together. Cliff was just two years old, and Saskia was three. He held his little toy tyrannosaurus rex as we danced around the living room, and she twirled in her tutu and fairy wings. Alicia Keys' powerful voice filled the house, and I sang along as we danced and laughed.

For me to be dancing with my children was something of a miracle. I had been so sick for the first three years of motherhood. Periods where I was so weak and bed-bound, unable to hold my children, walk down the street with them, let alone dance with them. I used to lay unwell, in pain, on the couch, while the various babysitters we called in would play with them on the floor or carry them to the bath. To now be twirling, leaping, singing and laughing was beyond anything I could hope for. It brought us all so much joy.

I could feel his shadow behind me on the staircase. Unhappiness hovering. I looked to meet his five o'clock shadow, downturned mouth and disapproving eyes. "Turn it down. I'm working. Take them outside."

I did take them outside. And we danced by the pool, swam, threw the ball and snuggled on the pool lounger, taking selfies. I was determined not to let Joseph's disapproving gaze interrupt our fun.

It became a repeated event. When feeling well, I could be quite a fun mama. From playing instruments, to water fights, singing songs, playing dress-ups and speaking in made-up languages. There were times when I would get quite raucous, my inner child coming out to play with my little peeps. And every time I accessed this unbridled joy, it would be met with Joseph's disapproval and some request to pack it away again. To mute myself.

I tried inviting Joseph to join in our fun and games, but that made him even more annoyed, and he'd offer some excuse. Work. Tired. Hungry. It was all too much for him so he would retract into himself. Go to his man cave. And the kids and I would carry on.

Joseph would poke his head out in moments of quiet, calm, sadness, distress or screen time. He could engage with us then. But all the life, the laughter, the play... it was just too much for him. He was happier, it seemed, when I existed in a state of misery.

And on one such day, dancing in the living room, I realized that my playful joyful self would never be welcome with him. That it never had been. That I had packed it away so tightly that I'd forgotten it was there altogether. That I wanted to dance and sing and play so much. That I simply would not quiet myself anymore, simply to receive his specific brand of love.

As the song flicked over to a Spice Girls track, I started having flashbacks. All the moments of sympathy and care that had come when I was hurting, weeping, angry. And all the glares, withdrawals, passive aggressive comments that had come when I dared to play, to dance, to sing, to joke. The flashbacks went back past my relationship with Joseph, and I saw images of my mother, my father. Telling me to be quiet. To shut up. Go to my room. To turn the music down. Stop dancing. Stop being silly. And my mother's pitiful voice, "I'm so sad for you." The kind of warped validation she would offer when I was having a hard time. The presents she'd bring me. Bags and bags of clothes. The only way she could love me. To meet me in my sorrow. In my pain. And band-aid it away with pity and presents.

I had learned that love comes with pain and presents... or not at all.

Cliff's little hand roused me from my remembering, tugging my harem pants. "Mama, huggie!" He looked up with his round face and innocent eyes. And I scooped him up into my arms, flew him over to the sofa, placed him down and proceeded to blow big juicy raspberries on his pale little belly. He squealed with delight. The abandoned laughter of a child who knows his joy is welcome in the world.

That moment, although seemingly small, was one of the first times I realized that my marriage might come to an end. There had been no laughter for over a decade. And I had so much laughing to do. Without knowing it, I had neglected my playful parts to be held in his arms. And I knew this was no longer a sustainable choice.

A Tout a l'heure

Drawn into your

Process

Again.

Finding myself

Leaking energy

Just to make it

Safe

For you to lean in

And love me

Even for a

Moment.

I've been here

A thousand times.

Your therapist

Your mother

Telling myself

That my

Reflections

Are needed

And some kind of

Self-validating

Badge of

Consciousness.

"I'm not like

The other women"

I hear myself utter

Again

To some new

Basket case of a man

Who can't get his

Monster

In check

Or unfurl

The fingers of his own

Fear

Choking his heart

That clearly

Yearns for me.

When did I

Take on

The impossible task

Of taking your fear

Away?

Was it to bolster

My own

Bruised ego

Or am I

More simply

Entangling myself

In your fear

As a futile distraction

Instead of embodying

My own

Splendid mastery?

The world is waiting

For me

To grace it

With my magic

But I keep

Finding my way

Back

To your fear

Wrestling

With your sleeping

Grandeur.

It's getting

Quicker and quicker

To remember

That your battles

Are not mine

To fight

Your fear

Is not mine

To metabolize.

So I let go

Each time

With more ease

More grace

Finding my freedom

Finding my form

And refocusing

On all the gifts

I have to bestow

On this earth.

Enjoy your process

Darling

I'll be dancing

In the sunshine

Come join me

Anytime.

A tout a l'heure, mon amour

Viens, quand to veux.

The lure of the unavailable man is like crack for neglected girls. We remain poised, tongues hanging out, waiting to lap up the lines of love powder that they sparingly sprinkle out for us. And the more hooked we become, the sparser the offerings of love, care, bare minimum attention become.

Of course, we never realize we're stepping into the same hell of unavailability, until we are already in it. Strung out. Starving. Aching for a hit from some guy we barely know but imagine to be the remedy to the unprocessed pain of our past. Little girls prancing into projections that take us right back to our neglectful origins. Then we convince ourselves that we can make do with less. Excuse bad behavior. Stop breathing a word about it to our friends who become increasingly fed up that we have found ourselves back here again. Distressed and deprived.

And back here again is exactly where I found myself with Lucas. Even with all the therapy and healing that had happened after my divorce and my awful relationship with Harley, I was still prone to plunging myself into fairytales that could never be lived.

The moment I crossed the boundary from friendship to being one of Lucas's many lovers, I had already bridged into the world of self-abandonment that was so familiar to me. This time, I didn't give up my playfulness, like I did with Joseph. In fact, our dynamic was abundant with play. Perhaps that's part of what made it so delicious.

That and his chiseled body and luscious lips.

What I did give up was my moral code, the knowing that non-monogamy didn't feel right for me. I wanted more than what he was ever going to give. And I went in anyway. Overriding my true wishes in favor for a series of sensual moments, deep soul-opening conversations, and a handful of mornings waking up with his stiff cock poking into my back and his tanned arms around me. Delicious delusion. He had been honest about what he was available for from the get-go. I'd met him at a sex party for fuck's sake. I'd laid spooning with him while he talked about his various sex buddies. It was me who had been dishonest. With him and with myself.

I'd also seemed to have taken on the role of his advisor, coach, therapist or, dare I say it, mummy. It had started before we crossed into lover land. We'd be laying there chatting and he'd tell me about some drama he was having with one of his women. Like he was aching for advice, or an ally, or something to satisfy or soothe him. And I stepped into that role of wise woman, as is so damn easy for me to do. My therapist hat would slip on silently and swiftly.

It was only later that I learned that every time I said yes to this role that was so often open and aching to be filled, I made it impossible to be loved. Impossible to be met. Instead, I became a servant. Useful. But also, the potential server of shame, the one thing we never want to receive from our partner. It was me, again, giving up any potential of intimacy. Abandoning it by stepping onto a pedestal where I felt safer. Needed. Useful.

So, there we were, casually connecting on every level, with me twisting myself into knots trying to keep a connection that was tearing me apart. Because I wanted more. So much more.

"Tell him the truth," encouraged the ever-earnest Esther after yoga class one evening. "I was thinking about it in Savasana. If you want more, tell him. Keeping things as they are is making you so anxious and so, so sad. You've been like this for months now. It's no good. Either he will surprise you and say he feels the same way, or he will tell you he doesn't. And then you have to decide if you want to continue or end it."

"I can't imagine my life without him," I exclaimed. "And I don't think we can go back to being just friends. There's just too much chemistry. But you're right. I'm in knots about this every single day. I hate the thought of him with other women. And it's not good for me that, for one week it's like our souls are intertwined, and then he goes silent or tells me he's focusing with another lover for a while. It's so destabilizing." Then I added, "By the way, you're not meant to be thinking about my love life when you're on the yoga mat, silly." And we both giggled a bit, breaking the tension of the moment.

"I'm not sure that's a very conscious way to go about ethical non-monogamy. You know I have been dating this couple for a while now, and while I am no expert on the topic, it seems to be all about communication, consistency and making each other feel safe and validated. It doesn't sound like he's doing that at all."

"You're right. It does seem to be when and how he wants it. There's no consistency, and it's like I'm grateful when he's available, but I just have to put up with it when he's not."

Esther looked at me with pure and serious eyes and said, "Communicate, communicate, communicate. It's the only way."

She was right. So, I worked up the courage to bring it up with Lucas at our next connection time. He didn't even like to call them dates. He said the word was too loaded and formal. I had been practicing what I was going to say in the mirror for a few days prior to our meeting. My anxiety was through the roof. What would happen if he didn't feel the same way? To be honest, I was pretty sure he didn't, but clarity was important. Something needed to shift.

After a particularly satisfying sex session, Lucas and I lay body to body, sweaty and moist, regaining our breath. I felt pangs in my heart. I felt so much for this man. I felt so open with him. Playful, free and relaxed. But it was in this space the anxiety and confusion bubbled, more and more as we continued our lusty journey.

"Lucas, I love our time together," I began and placed my hand over his heart.

"So do I. We are fucking epic together," he replied.

A smile creeped into the corner of my lips. I took a long breath. "I want more." There, I'd said it. No bells and whistles, just the honest truth. I held my breath waiting for his reply.

"I'll give you more, girl. Do you want to hop on top or fancy a spoon session? What does the lady desire?"

I was momentarily taken aback, then realized of course that's what he thought I meant. I tried to stay with the playful energy but bring the conversation to the deeper place I wanted to explore with him. "I'll fuck you ten more times in a minute," I said with a smile, "but I mean, I want to be with you, date you, maybe even be exclusive?" My voice went up at the end of the sentence, almost a squeak. "What do you think?"

His body braced; he pulled his hands off me and scooted back a bit. The three centimeters of space felt like a bottomless dark canyon separating us. "You know I don't date or do monogamy, Lena." He was right, I did know. But I winced, hearing him speak his truth. He sensed my pain and reached out to stroke my hair. "*Ma belle, je t'aime.* I love you. I love everything about you. You make my life so much better. But I am just not the relationship type. Freedom is so important to me."

I took a moment to muster up my words as I closed my eyes and leaned into his hand that was gently stroking my hair. I felt like a little kitten who just wanted to be patted and fed. "*Je t'aime mon amour.* I love you, too. We could have everything together. I feel so good with you. But the inconsistency, the highs and lows, it's not good for me. It hurts me. It's draining me."

His energy switched in a flash. "You knew what you were getting yourself into. It was you who crossed the line of friendship. Not me. I was respecting you. How dare you make me feel like my needs and choices aren't valid here?"

I was momentarily shocked by the ferocity and meanness that was emanating from his body. And as was my way back then, I went into fawn mode and tried to calm him down. "I'm sorry. You're right. It's my fault. I'm sorry. I'm sorry." I reached out to touch his arm.

He immediately softened and traced the line of my breast and leaned forward to kiss my pink nipple. "So, we just keep things as they are then?"

I rolled towards him and buried my head in his chest. "No," I whispered. "I can't." Tears sprung from the corners of my eyes as I realized that this conversation was not going to go my way. I had to give up this man who bought me so much joy and satisfaction, but also so much distress and anguish.

"But I want you in my life," Lucas countered. "You're so caring and so wise and you make me feel like I've got someone in my corner, someone to turn to."

Hearing this sparked anger in my belly. And I let it speak with kindness. "I have been that for you. A constant. A confidant. Always ready to love and care for you with open arms. But you don't offer me the same. There's no reciprocity here. And I'm not okay with that anymore."

I could see he was escalating, clearly distressed at the thought of losing the emotional support I was offering him. "I'm not ready. I'm scared. Relationships always end in pain. I've got too much trauma. I will hurt you. Or you'll hurt me. And it will just be a mess. Love is pain, Lena."

It was some kind of breakthrough for him to express his fear so honestly, rather than hide it under stories of freedom and lust. And a past version of me would have leapt into the role of soother and therapist. Tried to make it all better. Stayed where I was. Helped him process his pain. Tried to give him a different relational experience. And that same version of me would have become depleted, resentful and still devoid of the intimacy and reciprocity I really wanted. In that moment, I decided it was time for a breakthrough of my own.

"I know you're not ready. I know you're scared. Maybe it's time you figure it out. But I can't stay and be your lover slash therapist while you do. I really think I love you, but I don't want the kind of love that comes and goes and fucking hurts all the time." We lay opposite each other, silent for a while, staring into each other's eyes, knowing it was over. "I'll always love you, but for now, it needs to be from a distance. I know you've got some processing to do. I can feel it. Maybe one day, you'll be ready. And I welcome you to knock on my door when you do."

Tears were running down his cheeks. I'd never seen him cry before. And every cell in my body wanted to reach for him and scoop him into my arms and cover him in kisses. Just like a mother would a son, I realized. And with that moment of internal epiphany and disdain, I leaned forward and gave him a peck on the cheek and then pulled back and got out of his bed.

I stood naked, facing him silently for a while. Fuck, I was going to miss this man. I slid on my long black dress and slipped my matching red bra and panties into my bag. *"A tout a l'heure,"* I said. Then I turned and left his studio.

As soon as I got into my car, the tears flowed like a harrowing storm. "You did the right thing, Lena," I coached myself.

"Maybe he will come after you," piped up another deluded part of me.

"He won't," I countered.

"Maybe he will do some healing work and come find you when he is ready," offered the same naïve aspect of me.

I wiped my tears away, tucked my bedhead hair behind my ears, put on my oversized black Gucci sunglasses, and took a moment to gather myself. "This is me saying no to self-abandonment. This is me choosing my healing."

The Last One

You were the last one

The last one to lead me

Into the hell of

Unavailability

The place where I wanted to

Grab and hold and twist

Into the easiest

Unneediest

Version of myself

So you'd occasionally

Sprinkle my tongue

With your speedy

Love drug.

I had thought

You would be my

Ever after

The last man who would

Enter my body

My being.

I wanted you like I'd never wanted any other man.

And your dangerous

Pseudo quasi half-conscious state

Had me convinced

There was enough energy

To create the crucible

For it to be true.

So, I held the space

A little while

Coaxing you in

Through the gift of

Spaciousness.

Fooling myself

That this was an

Enlightened move

But really

It was the same old

Tortured witchery

The fucked up

False-love tarot

Of traumatized girls.

I eroded my spirit

In the process

Metabolizing your fear

On your behalf

But one morning

I looked in the mirror

At my tearstained face

And my tummy

Hollow with distress

And I realized

That you were not

The last man for me

You were the last

Lost boy

Whose hand I would hold

The last patient

I would bandage up

With my own wounds

The last trick of the light

The last intergenerational

Burden

I would pick up and place

Inside my own chest.

I did not let you

Break my heart

Like the others

Instead, I broke my own

To liberate myself

From the old stories I carried

And reorient to something new.

Goodbye, beautiful man.

Thank you for being my saltiest, sweetest, last.

I'll taste you forever.

We all want to believe in the goodness of humans. That people can change. Even when the evidence shows us otherwise. There's an innocence to this. A beautiful innocence. And it's often not until we've trusted and been burned one too many times that our caution kicks in. Some may call it pessimism. Jadedness. Others may call it maturity. A healthy form of protection in a world full of tricksters. Smoke and mirrors. Men and women full of unconscious wounding.

Even after everything I had been through, I still held a rather innocent heart. If my heart had eyes, they would be big clear baby blues with long eyelashes that bat, unperturbed by wolves in sheep's clothing. If my heart had hands, they would still reach out and take candy from strangers. Because why not accept gifts from strange men? Innocent or traumatized? I suppose the label doesn't matter. The point is, I wanted so much to trust words, promises and those little moments that seed future fantasies, full of happiness.

So when Lucas reappeared with what seemed to be his heart on his sleeve, I leapt right in despite the warnings of my friends.

It was a boringly normal Wednesday. I was home seeing clients online and planned to go for a beach walk and yoga in the evening. Work and self-care. Standard stuff. I had taken time off from dating after the heartbreak of ending things with Lucas. I needed recovery time. It had been about a month, and I was doing the right thing by filling my days with girlfriends, exercise, lots of cuddles and fun activities with the kids, gym, yoga. You name it. I was doing it. Getting over it. Life-ing. With my big girl pants on, as Ellen would say.

After my last client session ended, I put some music on—Florence and the Machine today. And rolled out my yoga mat to stretch. As I got into downward dog, my buzzer rang. I wasn't expecting anyone and assumed it must be a visitor for another unit.

"Hello, who are you here to see?" I asked as I pressed the intercom.

"Delivery for Lena," replied the formless voice.

"Okay, wow. Come up!" I rarely received deliveries. If I did, it was some electronic object or obscure homeware item I'd ordered on Amazon or some delicious food delivery when I didn't have it in me to cook. But I hadn't ordered anything, so I was a little perturbed.

When I opened the door, a huge bouquet of peonies and eucalyptus springs were presented to me. It was quite stunning. My heart jumped a little. Who could these be from? There was no one in my relational field I could think of.

I thanked the delivery woman, closed the door, set the vase on the table and searched for the note. There was a gold envelope attached to the side of the vase. Curious, I opened it.

Ma cherie, Je ne peux pas vivre sans toi. Je T'aime, toujours.

Lucas

Lucas telling me he loves me and can't live without me was the last thing I expected. And I had very mixed feelings. It had taken so many tears and so much processing to get over the heartbreak of him not wanting me the way I wanted him. And I was only recently recalibrating. Now this.

Then again, this was so romantic, so sweet. The stuff of movies. I wanted that. I daydreamed of this kind of thing happening all the time. And it was my gorgeous Lucas. We had been so special together. What if he did just need some space to see how wonderful I was, how wonderful we were?

In a split second, I conjured up a potential timeline where we lived happily ever after. I'd move into his studio. He'd sculpt, and I'd write and then we would take creative breaks and fuck for hours. After, he'd cook me grilled cheese sandwiches ('cause that seems to happen in every American romcom) and we would lay together and watch the sunset out the window as he stroked my hair.

Delusion alert! I caught myself in the pretty Hollywood reverie. *But what if you really could have that?* a small voice piped up inside me. The same voice that had told me he might come back when I sat crying in my car after he rejected me. What if this little voice was right?

In the past, this inner voice of mine, the sweet sound of my small abandoned inner child, had a habit of taking me towards the wrong men. The ones who could not love me well. And I had learned to set boundaries with her. She was the voice that encouraged me to accept less, do more and make excuses for bad behavior. My little neglected girl. All she really wanted was to be wrapped up and held and whispered to, like a little baby. I'd done a lot of parts work in therapy around her and found ways to soothe her through accessing healing touch modalities like massage and craniosacral therapy and foot reflexology. Or I used things like weighted blankets and sitting in flower baths to make her feel safe and happy.

Yet she sounded different this time. She wasn't convincing me to accept less or sing for my supper of sex and cuddles. She was suggesting I give him a chance to show me he loved me. To see if words and actions lined up. This sounded reasonable. And as I began to accept her suggestion, the fantasy of a future with Lucas became a little more vivid in my imagination, rather than just a momentary mirage.

As I sat, smelled the flowers and smiled, my phone beeped with a message. It was Lucas.

Ma Cherie, I hope you like the flowers. Meet me at the beach at seven pm? I will bring us a picnic dinner.

Fuck, he knew how to get me. Picnic dates were, and still are, a major turn on for me. They are the best kind of non-physical foreplay in my book. The care it takes to pack up a feast and then lay it out. The soft blanket. Mother nature all around. And two bodies that often end up snuggled up. Something about the combination of these things ticked all my boxes. I could feel myself getting giddy with excitement. Of course I was going to go. To lean in. It was Lucas.

But I could feel myself becoming a bit airy, ungrounded and less integrated than I'd like, so I decided to call my angel and devil besties for a moment of grounding and balance. I put them on a three way video call. Ellen was in the Bahamas at her beach house and Charlie was in Amsterdam for some DJ event. But as fate would have it, they both picked up.

My whole body felt more safe and solid as soon as I saw these two women. I knew no matter what happened, they would be there for me.

"Hey, girl, what's up?" Charlie greeted me.

"Good morning, beautiful ladies," chimed Ellen.

"So... Look!" I turned the phone to show them the flowers.

"Ooooh, pretty. Who are they from?" asked Ellen.

"Yeah, spill," said Charlie.

"They're from Lucas," I answered.

"So sweet. Go Lucas," said Charlie.

"No, uh-uh, absolutely not," chided Ellen. "What? He thinks that flowers and a note make up for how he treated you? Don't be fooled, Lena. He is trouble. Trouble. Trouble. Trouble."

I could feel myself contracting into my solar plexus and goosebumps appeared on my arms and the hairs stood up. A little bit of shame. "I'm meeting him at the beach for a picnic at seven," I said sheepishly.

"Oh my god, girl, you're asking for trouble. He is not your guy. He is a silly game playing wreck of a man. You should not be entertaining this. But okay, were you calling for permission?" Ellen was visibly pissed off. And for a moment, I was lost for words.

Charlie stepped in. "Lena, go on your picnic and have a wonderful time. Lap up the attention but stay grounded. You're information gathering, ok? Don't get lost in the fantasy but enjoy the moment. That's what life is about."

"You're always encouraging her to be reckless with her heart," countered Ellen. "You may like being single and fucking around, but that's not what Lena wants. Right, sweetheart? You want a relationship. And this guy isn't the guy that's going to give it to you."

I could feel the tension between my angel and devil. And instead of feeling calmer, I felt stressed and ashamed about what I was about to do—make love to the handsome yet emotionally unavailable Lucas, all night. To give him the power to shatter my heart all over again.

"What if he's changed? What if he just needed some time without me, to realize how important I am to him?" I piped up. That same little abandoned girl voice finding expression.

"Exactly darling," affirmed Charlie. "Give him a chance to show you, not tell you."

"I don't think people change like that. But it seems you're not looking for advice. You've already made up your mind. So, yeah. Let us know how it goes. Sorry for being harsh, but I've been around the block a few times, and I don't like how this guy treated your heart. I want you to be with the right person. But enjoy the picnic, I guess."

Charlie swiftly redirected the conversation. "What are you wearing, babe?"

"I hadn't thought about it yet. I called you both right away. I think maybe denim shorts, a plunging body suit and a kimono. What do you think? Hair down and messy? Like I haven't thought about it too much... but really have."

They both giggled. "Perfect," said Charlie. "Go and report back after."

"You always look gorgeous. Send me a photo of your outfit. Love you, even when I don't agree with you," added Ellen.

"I love you both. Wish me luck." I ended the call, looked at the flowers one more time and sent Lucas a text.

See you at seven. xxx The flowers are gorgeous. Thank you.

A shiver of anticipation went through my body. I took a deep breath and flicked my music over to Ben Howard to give me chill vibes while I got ready for the date.

As I walked down the hill to the beach, I could see him waiting for me. He'd set up the cutest picnic with a rug, round cushions and a Moroccan style throw. And there was a picnic basket and a bottle of pink prosecco (he knew it was my favorite seaside drink) chilling in an ice bucket.

He was wearing loose white linen pants and a light blue cotton shirt held closed by only one button at his core. As I approached him, he lifted his aviator sunglasses, smiled wide and reached his arms out wide to receive me. "Lena, *ma belle*! How I have missed you. Come here."

He pulled me into his arms, and I nuzzled my head into his familiar chest. He kissed my hair a few times, then lifted my chin so our eyes could meet. God, I was such a goner. Then and there, I was totally his. "Thank you for the beautiful flowers," I said.

He leant down and kissed me, at first softly, then deeply. With all the unspoken feelings speaking through his lips, his tongue and his roaming hands. After a while, we settled down on the picnic rug and he poured me a glass of pink prosecco. "To us," he toasted.

I clinked his glass with mine, but I queried the toast. "To us? What about us?"

Lucas frowned. "I'm so sorry I pushed you away. I haven't been able to get you out of my mind for the last month. And no matter who I try to distract myself with, all I want is you. You mean everything to me. I love you."

I was a little put off by his expression and became defensive. "Lucas, we've already been through this. I don't want to be one of many women you're fucking. I don't care if you love me if you're not able to love me exclusively." My whole body braced, and I felt hot with frustration.

He reached forward and touched my cheek. "What I am trying to say is that I want to try with you. Exclusivity. You're worth it. This is really big for me. Do you understand?"

"Oh," I replied, not knowing what to say.

He went on. "I've been thinking a lot about it, and I think it's time I grow up. And be serious. To try having a relationship. I know you are the right person to do it with. There's no one else I'd want to go through the highs and lows of it all with. Only you."

Again, I got a weird feeling in the pit of my belly. Something didn't feel right. He wanted to 'try it out' or 'practice' with me. But as he continued to stroke my cheek and look at me with his fucking sexy face, that little neglected girl inside me whispered *Lean in, Lena. He's showing you he cares. Receive, receive.* And so, I did.

We spent about an hour kissing and cuddling, sipping prosecco and watching the sunset. And then I got the courage up to ask, "So what does this mean? What happens now?"

"Well, you're my girlfriend now, *Cherie*. And I am your *petit copin. Voila!*"

My heart skipped a beat. But I needed more information. "But what does that look like? No other women? Are you sure you can do that? That you want to do that?"

"Shhhh." He placed a finger over my lips, then leaned down to kiss them softly and quiet my line of inquiry in the process. "We have time to figure everything out. For now, let's go to your place. I want to be naked with you and fuck you all night long."

There was no arguing with that. His certainty in the matter had my pussy on fire in an instant. We packed up and did as he suggested. We were so in tune sexually that night it felt like we were sending ripples of love out through all of humanity. Healing the world, one thrust at a time.

The next morning, I found myself in the same position as I had been a month ago. His arms around me, the big spoon with his delightfully above-average cock pressed into me. And for a moment, I had a flash of fear. What if it was just an act? What if it wasn't real? What if he was going to break my heart all over again? I could feel him rouse and kiss the back of my neck and give good morning kisses all the way down my spine. "*Bon matin,* my girlfriend," he whispered then rolled me over and buried his head between my legs. A breakfast of champions. Thirty minutes and four orgasms later, he lifted his head and said, "I am so happy here with you, but I need to go. I have an appointment. See you for dinner?"

I nodded, grinning like a cheshire cat.

For a few weeks, it felt like I was living in a waking fantasy. Lucas came over nearly every night (when the kids weren't with me). We ate together, talked for hours, fucked for even more hours. I felt so loved up. All doubts I had about things not working out had vanished. Until one Friday evening, he went silent. Stone cold silent. We'd had plans to meet for a late supper and a sleepover as I was spending the afternoon with my children.

I hadn't heard from him all day, which was strange. I'd messaged him just before three pm before collecting the kids from school and had no reply. By seven-thirty when I dropped the kids at their dad's, my anxiety had spiked and I'd made up a thousand stories ranging from him having an accident to him deciding he was done with me and never wanted to talk to me again. At eight pm, I messaged him again and checked in.

Is everything ok? Still on for nine pm at my place?

Nothing. I sat glued to my phone until one am. Nothing. He hadn't even read the message. After a fitful few hours of sleep, I checked the phone. Still nothing. It was torture.

And the torture continued for five days. Silence. The ultimate punishment for any of us with history of neglect or parents who withdrew love as some kind of psychological punishment. I went straight to self-pathology. What had I done wrong? Had I said something? Smelled bad? What had caused him to pull away?

I had made a rule for myself some years back that I would not follow anyone I was dating on social media. It was a recipe for anxiety, projection and nothing good. But after five days of trying my best to stick to my rule, I broke it and looked at his Instagram. And there he was, sharing stories of his sculptures and out partying with his artist friends the night prior.

Blinding.

White.

Rage.

Usually, I would have enough containment to stop myself from communicating in a reactive state, but I was too far gone. I sent a voice note to his Instagram messages:

Lucas, what the fuck? You're ghosting me? You're out partying and leaving me wondering if you're dead in a gutter? What is wrong with you and how could you do this to me?

And then another one: *Lucas, honey, what happened, did I do something wrong?*

And then another one: *Please, just let me know you're okay, even if you don't want to be with me anymore.*

Oh, my goodness. He'd turned me into a crazy fragmented traumatized mess. This wasn't how I wanted to feel.

I called Charlie, sniveling. "He ghosted me. He hasn't been in touch in five days. He's out partying and probably fucking a million bitches."

"Aw, babe, what a fuckhead. I'm sorry. How dare he treat my peeps like that? I want to smash his head in," Charlie replied.

I laughed a little as snot ran from my nose to my lips. I grabbed a tissue and blew hard, salty tears and snot filling it up. "I don't know what to do now. Why is this happening?" I cried.

Charlie and I talked for about an hour, and we agreed I should do nothing and see what he did next, if anything at all. She was all about information gathering.

Later that evening, as I was making a spaghetti bolognaise, my favorite comfort food, Lucas opened the door and came into the kitchen. I'd given him a key two weeks prior.

I was initially startled, then mad, then confused, and I couldn't help it. I started crying, wooden spoon in hand.

"I'm sorry, I'm sorry." He came and put his arms around me and kissed away my tears "I freaked out. I got scared. I shut down. I'm an asshole. You deserve better."

I nodded, still sobbing and unable to find words.

He took me in his arms, stroked my hair and turned off the stove. He silently led me to the bedroom, undressed me, and we made our most luscious love to date. Make up sex with the scent of bolognaise and tears in the air.

That was the beginning of a series of highs and lows over the next six months. We'd have a few weeks of bliss and then he'd go quiet again. Disappear. Leave me like a strung-out crazy person, then reappear with excuses, apologies and more orgasms to keep me hooked. And I let it happen. My neglected little girl was addicted to the high-low cycle and expertly convinced me Lucas was my soul mate, and if I gave it time, he'd move through his fears and stop running away.

I'd stopped talking about the highs and lows so much to Ellen because I knew she'd get on my case about it which meant we grew a little distant over the period. I missed her terribly.

The final act of abandonment and betrayal happened the day after Lucas and I got back from a long weekend together. We'd spent a weekend at Byron Bay, swimming, listening to live music and fucking like rabbits. On the last day, Lucas asked me to move in with him. This was big. A dream come true. This had to be the shift I was waiting for. He couldn't go silent on me if we were living together. I'd told him I'd love to, but we would need to talk more about my kids. He'd met them twice, but he didn't have a relationship with them, and I couldn't fully imagine him being part of their lives, our lives. This had always been one thing that had caused me pause with Lucas. A big red flag. But I'd continued to ignore it, because I felt so darn good with him.

When we got back from the airport, we shared a taxi back. It dropped him off first and at his house, I got out and kissed him tenderly. "Thanks for an amazing weekend away together. I love you so much and I can't wait to live with you. We're going to have a beautiful life together, my love."

He stayed silent and looked at me with a kind of intensity I couldn't quite place. Perhaps a flash of fear. "*Bon nuit*, Lena. *A demain*." We'd arranged that I'd come over the following morning to talk about the kids and what it would look like to live together.

That night, I let myself get lost in the dream of what life living with Lucas would be like. I'd imagined it many times before, but this time, it was with the knowledge that it was really going to happen. I went about unpacking, washing and settling, singing at the top of my lungs. Happy. Hopeful.

The next day, on the way to Lucas' studio, I stopped to pick us up some piping hot almond flat whites and his favorite almond croissants. His door was always unlocked. It was part of his mission to live freely. So, I turned the knob and entered. I could hear Kings of Leon playing in his studio and walked towards the music.

My body responded before my eyes and my mind could catch up. There on the floor were three naked bodies fucking. Lucas and two of his young French artist female friends. I dropped the coffees and croissants to the floor, frozen in disbelief. But also, there was a small part of me that thought, *This was bound to happen, Lena. It was only a matter of time.*

The girls looked up before he did. One of them smiled smugly at me. I recognized Katerina, who had been lusting after him the whole time we were together. She stared into my eyes with a devilish glee, clinging on to him while he penetrated her. The other girl, Nora, who was behind him, noticed the shift in energy and turned around to see me. "Oh, *merde*, fuck", she said and pulled out of the threesome. Katerina's gaze remained on mine.

Lucas turned his head to see me. But his expression didn't change. He pushed Katerina off him and said, "Girls, get out." He lay down on the cold studio floor, staring into space as they scrambled to grab their clothes and scoot out.

I stood there, unable to speak or move. It was like we were both immobilized in time. After a while, he turned his head to look at me and simply said, "So?"

"So? Are you fucking kidding me? You asked me to move in with you last night. So? So, you go fuck two dumb young French bitches? I don't understand, Lucas."

"I think I got scared again," he said. "It happens. I still want you to move in with me. I love you."

Even my traumatized inner child knew this was not okay. All parts of me were a united front. For the first time ever. Unfortunately, it took this horrible moment to make it happen.

"Stay the fuck out of my life," I said quietly. "I have loved you like no one else. And I know you love me too. But you are too damaged. It's over."

I turned and left. Instead of going home, I drove to Naomi's serviced apartment. She was in town for a month, and I didn't want to be alone. As soon as she opened the door, I flung myself into her arms. "It's over. It's over. For good this time."

Naomi made me a cup of chamomile tea, ran me a bath and buzzed for some extra towels and blankets from reception. She was such a good friend. Arms always open wide when I couldn't tolerate my aloneness. I recounted the whole sorry story to her. I could feel her having a lot of thoughts, but she refrained from any kind of 'I told you so' shaming or trying to coach me out of it. She simply said. "He's a fucker of a man, Lena. You deserve so much more."

Lucas was the last man I let sweep me up into his drama. The last man I went hard and fast with. Or at least, the last one for a while...

And that little neglected girl inside me? She grew up, just a little. Or perhaps, I learned to catch her when she posed as the voice of love, light, consciousness and reason. Whatever psychological process was happening, I was learning not to abandon myself in the quest for love.

Sexless Or Reckless

Swinging

Back and forth

Between those

Gentle ones

Without a backbone

Who contort

Around my spine

But can never

Carry me

And those

Braced bastards

Who make me

Feel like a feather

But can snap me

Like a twig

And sometimes do.

The effeminate angels

Who turn me into

Some dickless man

Or the cocky cavemen

Who turn me into

A dainty doll

Or wretched rag.

My two-step dance

Is some thankless

Maze

Where I keep

Getting stuck

Sexless or reckless

Legs closed tight

Or pried open so wide

I can't even feel them

Anymore.

So I sit still

For a while

Swaying my hips

In the wind

And ask myself

Why I keep

Choosing

These extremists

Who will never be able

To dance with my

Pink lips and

Pretty toenails.

In all honesty

I don't yet know.

So, I sip my

Americano

Apply my lip gloss again

And wait for the answers to come.

The journey to love can sometimes feel like a pendulum swaying out of control. Off the charts. The highs the lows. Flicking from one type of person to another yet ending up alone again. Without movement.

Blobbed at home on the couch with a giant bowl of pasta, an overgrown forest covering my cooch, swiping aimlessly. I seemed to go back and forth between being this awful kind of couch monster and a sex-crazed, sparkly dating diva. But even within both these polarities, there would be extremes of their own. Sometimes my cooch would feel peaceful, productive and exactly where I needed to be. Other times it would feel like the quicksand of loneliness, and I'd find myself desperate to get off, put a dress on and flash my sensual smile at any game asshole. Anyone, anyone, is there anyone out there?

When I was dating, I'd flip between two different types of men. Either I'd pick the gentle sweet kind, who would jump when I snapped my sassy fingers, or those who would shut me up with their hyper-masculine dominant ways. And in both cases, the shadow aspect of the dynamic would leave me feeling like something wasn't quite right. The gentler men would become toys. Human handbags. Servants. Pleasers. But they would lack initiative. Just like Joseph did all those years we were married. And it would be me doing the planning, producing, pushing and pulling. A she-man. And it wouldn't be long until I would get frustrated. Bored. Annoyed. There was a part of me that wanted to be led, directed, guided. To surrender to my man. The ultimate feminine reverie. And with these guys, I never could.

On the flip side, I would choose strong hunk type men who could make me wet with their sweet talk and expertly get my clothes off within only a couple of hours. In bed, I enjoyed exploring this submissive side of myself. Being thrown down, picked up and pushed against walls, maneuvered like a piece of pink saltwater taffy. But what would come with these men was often a complete inability to welcome my preferences, boundaries or emotions. And I don't mean in bed. They were all very good at listening to and respecting my sexual wishes and limits. It was out of bed where the responsiveness ended. If I wanted to choose the restaurant, change the day or time of our rendezvous, or chat about a particularly shitty day, I'd be met with resistance, annoyance, some snippy little shaming comment, or the blank stare that tells me he has vacated the emotional building.

Inevitably, neither type was right for me. Either way, I'd have to self-abandon. Let go of the desire (and dare I call it need?) to yield and be led. Or let go of the desire for attunement, emotional intimacy and equity.

One Tuesday in therapy, I was moaning to Tabitha about my conundrum. "Why do I keep choosing these polar opposites? Pushovers or playboys. I'm sooooo frustrated with myself!"

I wanted her to give me some clear attachment-based answer. A quick three step guide to choose the right man. Of course, therapy doesn't work like that. Instead, she pulled her glasses slightly lower down her nose and peered over them at me with a look that silently said, "Lena, you know you're not going to get the answer from me."

I pulled my bare feet up onto the couch and covered them with the familiar crochet blanket. I felt very young in that moment, as I often did in the delicate vulnerability that the therapy room offered me. "I just want a breakthrough. I am so sick of this. It's like I have to choose between going out and fucking the wrong men or not fucking anyone at all. Sometimes I sit in my bath and cry because I should be having so much more sex than I am right now. Perimenopause isn't far away, maybe it's already started for fucks sake, and I feel like time is running out. A different kind of biological clock. I just want to fuck my imaginary boyfriend every morning and night. Is that so much to ask?!" I exclaimed.

Tabitha chuckled a little and took a sip of tea. I mirrored her and sipped mine with a little bit of a self-deprecating snort. "Lena, you have this habit of being very all or nothing about dating. About many things, in fact. You're either guns blazing, eating men for breakfast, or you've deleted the apps and going on a dick diet." We laughed. "I wonder if the key to this supposed breakthrough you're seeking is in a little bit of continuity. Not quitting men every time you feel distressed. And not dating with such intensity after one of your 'man-fast' periods. What would it be like to slow down and watch your tendency to all or nothing behavior? You may find that it moves the needle with how much patience and curiosity you have with these men to begin with also. It's just a hypothesis... What do you think?"

I tried to digest her words and couldn't fully process them. What I could hear was the suggestion to slow down and stick with the process. "I need time to think about that. I guess I do have a habit to yo-yo date. It's like, no matter what I do, I abandon a certain need or desire, to fulfil another... or simply to protect my heart."

Tabitha spoke more sternly. "No man will ever meet all your needs. Perhaps this isn't only about self-abandonment; this may also be about maturity. There's a petulant child inside you, in fact many petulant children, who are all seeking soothing, satisfaction, freedom and fairytales. Mature love is about none of these. So, while you've been working on ending your self-abandonment tendencies, perhaps you're ready to move on to the next piece now."

I felt a little shamed by her comment and tone, yet I could feel the truth in what she was saying. I had worked so hard to get out of abusive, dismissive and neglectful dynamics. To find my peace, my power, my playfulness. Perhaps I didn't need to work so hard on that anymore. Perhaps it was time to stop dating like a woman healing from trauma and begin dating like a woman ready for next level love.

When we abandon parts of ourselves to be loved, we abandon love itself. The patience to sit with all parts of ourselves (no matter how wretched it feels) is the same patience that allows us to begin dating from a mature and compassionate heart.

Part 4 Overflowing Heart

Little Invitations

Lovely woman

I keep coming

Back here

Beyond

The intense longing

And epic grief.

These unfulfilled

Parts and places

That I keep

Forgetting

Are not yours

To fill up

Or tend to.

Lovely woman

I return to you

With the crash

Of each wave

On my shore

And all the

Jagged edges

The cliffs

Of my unconscious.

Return

Return

Return

To the safe pool

Hidden in the

Mountains

Of my heart.

To bathe

In the sacred

Waters

Pure molecular love

Reborn again and again.

Lovely woman

I remember

Who I am

Without the complex

Hustle

And dynamic

Struggle

Of this mad world.

Remember

Remember

Remember

Who I am

Beyond

The conditioned earth.

Little invitations

To meet here.

Sweet Babies

I've never felt this way before

She said to the narcissist

I've never felt this way before

She said to the married man

I've never felt this way before

She said to the spiritual fuckboy

I've never felt this way before

She said to the man who was doing his deep work but just
nowhere near ready.

But in fact, she had felt this way

Every

Single

Time.

The heaven-sent-eros-trauma-bond-type feeling

The you're-here-to-show-me a-new-kind-of-love-feeling

The I'll-never-be lonely-again-feeling.

And each time the feeling was a fucking lie.

Each time, the fragmented babies inside her

Were hoping the healing would be over

And that nirvana would begin.

And each time it got a little easier

To hold those little babies

In the arms of her inner elder

To become the missing matriarch

And curl up under her own safe wings

And build a nest

For the little babies to heal, grow and flourish

And keep them safe from those men

Who could not treat her with the care she deserved.

Gently, gently, my sweet babies.

Learning to love asks us to heal our trauma so we stop projecting happily ever afters onto the wrong people. But it's not easy to do. Not when we're wired for intensity, passion, and the heat of the moment. Not when we are skin hungry, starved of affection and just plain lonely. And oh, how I was hungry.

After the awful ending with Lucas, I did not take any time off dating. I was right back on the horse, riding men, left and right. It was some kind of unspoken revenge. I did not want to let him block or slow down my dating life. No fucking way.

There was Steve the suit.

Alex the builder.

Johnny the chef. And oh my, we did some creative things in the kitchen and the bedroom.

Bruno the pilot.

Sam the engineer.

Eli the lawyer.

And a few others, whose names I can't quite recall. Don't judge me. I was fucking my heart out to avoid feeling it.

I was also avoiding creative types. They had a habit of messing with me. I'd always be weak at the knees for them, and they were often hot messes who screamed trouble.

It never got past three dates. There was always something off. Either they'd mansplain me, bore me to tears, or I'd find myself choking on my spicy tuna roll at their patriarchal, racist, rude bullshit. Or the sex would suck. So, after three dates, it would be an amicable ending and I'd be on to the next one.

Then came Michael. I was gaga about him on date one. This never happened. Or at least, it hadn't in a while. Michael was a TV anchor on a local American TV station and flew to Singapore one week a month to visit his son, who lived there with his Singaporean mother, his ex. Michael was six-foot-four, had a perfect Californian accent and tan and dimples like Brandon from *Beverly Hills 90210*. My inner teenager wanted to put posters of him all over my bedroom wall, and write him love letters sprayed with cheap perfume and sealed with heart stickers. And my inner unexpressed performer wanted to put on ball gowns and walk some obscure red carpet with him. It helped that he was a total charmer, opening car doors, booking Michelin star restaurants, and expertly removing my Victoria's Secret panties with his teeth. I was totally his.

And while we hadn't talked about exclusivity, the future, or anything real at all, I had imagined it (like I always did).

"I've never felt this way before, Ellen," I shared on the phone while I was getting ready to meet him for drinks at C'est La Vie, a bar on the rooftop of the Marina Bay Sands. It was his last night in town, and I had planned to bring up the possibility of me flying to LA to spend some time with him the following month. I was a keen little kitten.

"You say that all the time," Ellen grounded me. Her words plunged me back into my body, and out of the mildly deluded fantasy I was in. Fuck, I think she is right. "Every three or four months, you meet someone who gives you the princess treatment and plenty of orgasms and you are immediately entranced. And none of them are husband material. Neither is this guy. He's all performance. He's got a four-year-old son in Singapore and an eighteen-month-old daughter in Orange County with two different baby mamas. You think you're going to be a priority? You think he's going to love your kids? He's here to wine and dine you and escape himself. He's not your guy."

He's not your guy. Ellen had said those four words to me countless times over the last few years. I needed to learn to pay attention to them. And stop falling for fake princes. "You're right," I whispered. "He's not my guy."

"It doesn't mean you can't have fun with him, honey. You're single. No shame in being wined and dined, but be grounded about it. Protect that precious heart of yours."

"Ok...." I was at a loss for words. I murmured something about having to go and ended the call.

I proceeded to get ready for the date. I wore my favorite asymmetrical white mini dress with one long floating sleeve, some red kitten heels and matching red lips. I scooped my hair up into a loose side bun over my open shoulder to balance the look and scooched on the tiniest nude lace G-string. And added some extra bronzer for good measure. Normally, I'd be wet from excitement, anticipating cross table foreplay and hours of pleasure. But this evening, I was lost in thought.

He's not my guy.

He's not my guy.

He's not my guy.

Ellen's words echoed. What the fuck was I doing? Could I really enjoy the evening and let him bury his face between my legs and enter me, now that I could see he didn't really care about me? This wasn't what I wanted. I wanted so, so, so much more. Not this.

I gave myself a stern look in the mirror. *Go have some fun, Lena*. I grabbed my vintage gold glow-mesh clutch and headed down to get my taxi to meet Michael.

As I arrived on the rooftop, our eyes met across the bar. I could tell he was delighted and aroused by my outfit. And as I strode towards him, I could feel my heart filling with tears that wanted to emerge. I swallowed hard and sucked them down.

"Hello, gorgeous," he greeted me. "You look absolutely smoking hot tonight."

"Thank you." I glimpsed away in a show of false modesty. I did look smoking hot. And I knew it. Usually when I was dressed like this, it was almost as if I was turning myself on and emitting a 'ready to rumble' and 'come fuck me' vibe. But tonight, I felt heavy, unexcited and almost repulsed. I did my best to hide it. He was the same Michael. It was me who had changed in a flash. He'd been honest about his situation from the beginning, and I had ignored what would be considered red flags for anyone looking for a relationship and marched forward into the role of mistress. Even though he was single, he was situationally unavailable.

As was his way, he ordered a bottle of wine and a range of appetizers. I loved when men ordered. It took small decisions off my often-overflowing plate. It let me relax. Feel like I was being looked after. And as I sensed my usual gratitude for his take-charge demeanor, I felt another swell of grief in my heart. I stuffed my face with a deconstructed vegetarian spring roll and gulped it down with the incredibly expensive Chablis that should never be drunk with such lack of appreciation.

For the next hour, I let Michael be the star of the show, which was his natural way anyway, and continued to stuff my face, to stuff down my grief.

He's not your guy.

He's not your guy.

I want my guy.

The fancy finger food was no longer able to muzzle my tears, so I excused myself, slipped off the high chair and found myself locked in the restroom cubicle weeping hard. I only gave myself three minutes, then peed for good measure, readjusted my dress then washed my hands and reapplied my Dior Red. I figured the best way to deal with my grief was to fuck it away. That's what I'd been doing since Lucas. I strode back to the table and walked up to Michael, pushed open his legs and stood between them, pressed up against his torso, ran my hands through his thick dark hair and whispered in his ear, "Take me home. It's time to get naked. I can't wait anymore."

He spluttered on his sip on wine and said, "Yes, Ma'am."

He swiftly signaled to the waiter, gave them his gold card, and within two minutes, we were in the elevator with his hand on my ass and kissing my neck. In the uber, I used my initiative and stroked his crotch, getting him ready for the instant we made it to his penthouse suite. He picked me up and placed me on the dinner table, pushed up my skirt and my G-string to the side. I hoped that each thrust would take my pain away, but it made it worse. Tears began to escape the corners of my eyes, and I was mortified.

To his credit, he noticed and paused to wipe them away and stroke my hair. "What's happening for you right now? Are you ok? Shall I stop?" I nodded. And then burst into tears. "What's wrong?" He was visibly distressed. He pulled my dress down, scooped me up and carried me to the sofa, then wrapped me in the cashmere throw that was resting on its arm. He put his arm around me and said, "Has something happened? I've never seen you like this." His show of empathy and care hurt my heart even more. He was a nice guy. He just wasn't my guy.

I decided to be honest. "Michael, I have had the most amazing time with you. You're charming, disgustingly good looking, an old school gentleman, clearly," I said, referring to the current scene we found ourselves in. "But today, I realized there's no potential for a relationship between us. Not a real one. I want to be more than a dazzling date one week a month. And I know you can't give me that. I'm not asking you to. But I want more. With someone else. So, I don't think I can carry on as we were. I wanted to keep it casual, but I like you too much. And I know it will block me from finding someone who can really show up for me."

He frowned and nodded in agreement. "You're right. I can't give you more than a few nights every time I visit. My life is too complicated. You are amazing. And selfishly, I'd love to keep our arrangement as it is. But I get it. You do deserve so much more. Thanks for being honest with me."

I leaned my head on his shoulder. "I guess I better go," I murmured.

"You don't have to rush out so fast. Why don't we have some dessert and cuddle a bit, say goodbye properly? We deserve at least that."

He was being so sweet. And I told him so. "I think that will just make it harder. I'm going to head home. I need a shower, a cry and a good sleep."

"As you wish. Let me call you a car." He walked me to the lobby, and as the car arrived, he took my face in his hands, looked in my eyes and said, "You are wonderful. I'll never forget you."

I didn't say anything. I couldn't. Instead, I smiled and shrugged my shoulders and slid into the backseat. As soon as the door closed, the tears flowed. And they flowed all through the night into the early hours of the morning. I fell asleep on my wet pillow and slipped into my dreamworld.

I dreamed I was sitting in an empty field. It was so expansive I couldn't see its edges. I was a young girl in the dream. Maybe six or seven. Wearing a pretty red smocked dress and my hair in plaits, with an uneven fringe and an overbite. To begin, the sun was shining, and I was happily playing with a wooden doll's house. But then the sky turned grey, and it got windy. I felt cold and realized I didn't have a cardigan and so I looked up in search of... someone. A grown up. To help. But there was nobody. I felt very small and alone. Helpless.

"Mummy," I called. "Mummy! Mummy!" Realizing that she wasn't there, I began to escalate, big juicy tears rolling down my plump cheeks. "I want my mummy."

All of a sudden, the field turned into a vast sand dune like something you'd see in a movie set in the Middle East. And I was in the body of my young adult self. Maybe twenty years old.

"What the fuck?" I thought mid dream, those moments where consciousness watches the vivid scene a little too closely. Several camels appeared over the crest of the sand peak, all ridden by purple hooded characters. As they rode towards me, I became quite terrified, but I didn't dare move.

"Mummy! I want Mummy," my seven-year-old voice whispered to my twenty-year-old self.

The camels formed a line before me and the purple hooded riders disembarked, standing by their animals, waiting for something. After a brief pause, the leader of the pack gestured to the others, and they removed their masks. The spectacle of my past boyfriends and lovers shocked me so much hot wet urine trickled down my leg. Then out of nowhere, a soft toy bunny appeared in my arms, and I clutched it tightly, wincing at the feeling of warm pee and the sense of shame.

The men's mouths opened in chorus. "Mummy! Mummy! She wants her mummy!" They repeated the phrase a few times and then erupted into laughter. As they cackled, I felt myself folding into myself like origami.

And then my eyes opened on my pillow. Awake in my bed. Thirty-seven years old. Dry panties. Thank goodness for that. As I took in the sunlight streaming through my bedroom window, I whispered to no one, "I do want my mummy," and wept.

After some time, in a bit of a haze, I brewed coffee in my rose gold French press and sat on the sofa with my journal. This dream needed some processing time. So, I wrote, and I wrote, and I wrote. The one sentence that was the big aha was "I have been burying myself in dynamics with men who can't love me to avoid grieving the feeling of being abandoned by my mother. It's time to process this."

I sent Tabitha a quick email. *Got time for a longer session next week please? I need to talk about my mother.*

Moats & Velvet

I pulled back

The love

That I had been

Pouring into you

And my huge heart

Was flooded

With a grief

So epic

Love with nowhere to go

Looking for a new destination.

So I built myself

A sacred moat

And soaked myself

In the ocean of it

Queen of my castle

Some kind

Of modern Rapunzel.

Yet in this new version

Of the fairytale

I stopped letting you hang

On my golden locks

I told you to go

Find the tools

To build yourself

Some kind of makeshift ladder.

Your climb

Up my tower

Must come

From your own labor.

I sat in the drawing room

With velvet pillows

Sunlight streaming in

Combing my precious hair

And holding my precious heart.

I invited all the ladies for tea

Each one kissed my cheek

Adjusted the crown upon my head

And reminded me

Of my precious fucking power.

When you decide to stop hiding from your grief, you'll need to learn to float in the ocean of it for a while. And call in the cavalry to bring you life rafts. And wine. And snacks.

So, that's exactly what I did. I took some time off dating (again) and really processed my maternal attachment trauma. The mother wound is a big one. It travels far and deep inside us. It seemed I had been using men to soothe or transfer my feelings. When I stopped, cold fucking turkey, it all came up. The grief. The rage. The loneliness. The hopelessness. Ugly crying. Pillow punching. Letter writing. Comfort food. I even started Muay Thai lessons. It was the best outlet for my repressed rage.

I'd meet my trainer once a week in my condo garden and punch it out. Kick it out. Blow off the steam that had been propelling me into the wrong relationships. That steam was all for my poor mother. My mother who did the best she could but simply couldn't get her own trauma in check to love me well. After each session, I'd feel so much space inside me. A weight off my shoulders. My jaw more relaxed. It was a good workout too and my ass and my little middle aged lady lower belly pouch thanked me. I was looking more toned than I had in years.

My girlfriends knew about my decision to pause dating and do some deeper processing and were in total support. They'd lovingly check in on me, almost like they'd coordinated it. Each day, I'd get a text or a call from someone. I was held in the net of their fierce feminine love.

I found myself with a lot of free time now that I wasn't wasting it on dud dates, or drama with all the wrong kind of men. In addition to doubling down on therapy (two sessions a week instead of one), I focused on my work. All that redirected energy started to pay off. I was booking speaking gigs and corporate programs around the world. And I'd started writing. Writing. Writing. Writing. A book was coming. Finally.

People had been asking me for a long time to write a book about healing, but I never felt ready. But suddenly, there I was, writing with my pot of tea each morning instead of ruminating over a man or what I was going to wear on whatever date I had planned that night.

I sent out a bunch of pitches to publishing houses one night. I received a bunch of rejections within a week. While I was a little disappointed, I kind of expected it. I was an unknown in the publishing world. But I knew I wanted to write the book anyway. It was coming through me at lightning speed. Deal or no deal. So, I wrote. Everything I understood as a 'patient-turned therapist'.

One Thursday, after Muay Thai practice, I sat down with my pot of tea to write a chapter or two. I opened my laptop to check my emails before diving into my creative time and there it was. An email with the subject: Publishing Offer. In disbelief, I clicked it open, and there was a brief but clear letter of offer. One of the biggest publishers in the world wanted to publish my book! I was stunned and took a few moments to collect myself. Then I had an impulse to call Lucas. We'd talked about me writing a book many times in our post-coital cuddle sessions. A stifled strange meow exited my mouth. I sounded like a cat in pain. I was filled with the polarizing sensations of jubilation and epic sadness. *I wish I had someone to share this life-changing news with. There's no one.*

I quickly corrected myself. "There may not be a man to share with but there are the most amazing women all around you who will be so excited for you... with you. In fact, the absence of all these stupid men is the reason you finally focused enough to get this deal in the first place."

I was impressed with my own pep talk. I went to look in the mirror, fluff my hair and apply some lipstick. "You're going to be a published author," I said to my reflection and did a little hip wiggle.

I picked up my phone and recorded a short video message to send to the girls' group chat. "Guess who just got a publishing offer? Me. Me. Me!!! Can you believe it? Thank you, my gorgeous women, for loving me through this time. You're all a part of this moment. So grateful for you."

I spent hours on the phone with each of my girls. I felt elated. Filled up. Loved. Hopeful. I hadn't felt this good in ages.

As I reread the email, I realized the deadline was only three months away. A little bit of panic crept up my spine. How was I going to swing that with my work schedule and being a present part-time mum? It felt like I needed to get away and focus on writing. Block out the rest of the noise and give this book my full attention. But I couldn't do that. Could I?

"Why can't you? Just go. Joseph would be happy to look after the kids. You know that. This is the opportunity of a lifetime," suggested Ellen. I gave her a thousand excuses. Mother guilt. Money. Work. "Excuses get you nowhere, love. This is an investment in your future. Invest in yourself. If you pick somewhere fabulous, I may even pack my suitcase and come with you. I could do with a bit of a trip."

"I think I want to write it in Italy," I replied. "I've had a thing for Italy forever, and I had three trips planned with three different men and they have all been cancelled. It feels like maybe I need to reclaim Italy as a man-free experience. What do you think?"

"I think Florence in November will be cute and cozy and inspiring. I'd meet you there for a bit if you go there. Florence is incredible."

"Let's do it," I confirmed. "I just need to get my ducks in a row first."

The first thing I did was discuss the idea with Joseph. He was more than happy to hold the fort with the kids while I was away for a month. He was such a loving father that he always embraced more time with his children. He was such a good co-parent that he would always support me in my life path, where possible. At times like this, I'd feel overcome with gratefulness for the role he played in my life. Next, I sat down with the children to float the idea of me being away. They were used to me travelling for work, so it didn't seem to bother them at all. I also reached out to a few of my mum friends and arranged some playdates for them while they were away. It felt as if I was being held in the loving net of my village.

I re-arranged my work schedule. Looked at my bank account and did some sums. There was no practical reason not to take this trip. Everything was planned and booked within a week of my chat with Ellen. Ten days later, I was on my way to my dreamy Italian writing trip.

I flew into Milan two weeks before Ellen was set to meet me in Florence. I'd planned three nights in a fancy spa hotel to decompress and then take the train to Florence and stay in a simple Airbnb in the old part of town. I had visions of living like a local. Buying fresh produce, cooking and eating on the little terrace and writing like crazy.

The hotel was divine. Old school Italian opulence everywhere you looked. A piano in the lounge, ornate chandeliers, a central courtyard covered in vines and flowers. And a decadent spa with everything you could ever imagine. I'd booked a massage and steam room session for the night of my arrival. As the therapist gently kneaded my post-flight back, the tears started to flow. And they did not stop. I expected that she'd seen similar shows of emotion on the massage table before. She expertly and sweetly continued her work while handing me a tissue. No words, no trying to make it better. Just support. It was exactly what I needed.

After an hour of weeping on the massage table, my face was puffy, and I felt tired. I sat in the steam room and let it work its magic. I was taking in deep exhales, and it felt like decades of stress and tension were leaving my body. Afterwards, I took a warm shower, bundled up in a hotel robe and climbed into the fluffy bed that was waiting for me. I didn't eat, didn't check my phone, just exited my wakefulness and all the emotion that went with it and entered a deep restorative sleep.

I spent three days repeating the ritual. Massage. Cry. Steam. Sleep. In the morning, I'd eat a decadent breakfast and do a workout, wander the streets of Milan for a bit and then return to the hotel for the evening self-care session. I needed it. I wasn't equipped to start writing yet. And I knew well enough not to force it. To take my time.

On the train to Florence, I opened my laptop, and the words began to flow. As the Italian landscapes whizzed by the train window, I barely noticed where I was, transfixed, inside my writing bubble. In no time at all, Florence was upon me. I dragged my suitcases off the train and realized I had no idea how to get to my Airbnb. Taking out my phone, I pulled up the address and set off along the cobbled streets.

After a few wrong turns, and a few pauses to give my hand a break from lugging my case, I arrived at the gorgeous old town, walked through the square and a little further to my Airbnb building where my host, Mario, was waiting outside. I must have stuck out like more tourists do in more local areas, and he bellowed "Lena, welcome to Florence. Let me assist you." He took my case and indicated for me to follow him into a very dark stairwell and up the stairs. "The lights are not working."

I felt somewhat uneasy walking up these spiraling dark stairs. Three stories. At the top, he took a moment to find the right key on his large jangling set and finally opened the old heavy brown door and switched on the lights. I gasped. The apartment was breathtaking. The front door opened into an open plan kitchen and dining room with arched windows that looked out over the old town towards the river that separated it from the main part of Florence. There was a small balcony with two chairs and a table—perfect for writing or a sunset wine. Off the living room was the first bedroom and up another small spiral staircase was a second loft bedroom, with a giant bathtub placed right next to the bed that looked out of another arched window towards the other direction, across the old town towards the hills. This would be my room.

Mario gave me some information on the apartment and the surrounding area and shortly after left. Instantly, I felt my aloneness. Tears pricked the corners of my eyes. What was I doing here? Away from my kids. My friends. My colleagues. *Come on, Lena, you're here to write your book. And Ellen is coming in two weeks. This is epic.* I tried to encourage myself, but it didn't work. I felt empty. Anxious. Lonely. Confused. Since it was about four o'clock in the afternoon, I decided to go and orient myself with the surrounding area.

I put on my green coat and made my way back down the winding dark staircase onto the cobbled streets. And I stood there at the bottom, the tears returned to the corners of my eyes. I sniffed a little and began to walk. Past a few small stores. The grocer. The ice creamery. The butcher. A trinkets store. Then I turned left and found myself back in the town square.

It was that odd time of autumn where it was beginning to get dark, and a haze was settling over the sky. There was a fountain in the middle of the square and a few people were perched on the edge, looking at their phones or rummaging in their bags. Mothers and children walked through the area, probably on their way home from school pickup, I thought. A few lovers sat on benches murmuring to each other. One couple making out with fervor and another older couple holding hands and watching the sky and the birds that were making their way to some destination in the most beautiful formation.

They would have been in their late seventies or early eighties. The woman had a knitted spearmint green hat on her head and a big woolly cream cardigan, baggy brown pants and old leather walking shoes. The man had on a tweed jacket, grey tracksuit pants and well-worn jogging shoes. In the hand that was not intertwined with his wife's (I just assumed they were married) he held a wooden walking cane with a rounded handle. They were a perfect pair. They looked so content. Sitting there. Together. Watching the birds. Welcoming the evening. Together.

A huge well of tears rose inside my chest and I couldn't hold it back. I started sobbing. Right there. On the street in Florence. I felt so lonely. I wanted a companion. I didn't want to be alone. My grief. It chose to make itself known in a new way. I felt somewhat self-conscious about my erupting tears, but I couldn't help it. So, I let it come. I found an empty bench to sit on, put my head in my hands and wept. In a similar but not so similar way to the dream I'd had where all my past lovers appeared, I started to see them flash through my mind. All these men that I'd been using to fill the void of my own loneliness. To stop myself processing this grief. Perhaps this is what Italy had in store for me, rather than writing my book, I mused. And then continued to cry.

After some time, I felt a gentle hand on my shoulder and was startled out of my process. *"Bella*, what's the matter?"

An older Italian man with a giant smile stood there, checking on my wellbeing. "I-I-I just arrived here, and I am all alone. And I feel... I feel... I feel overwhelmed," I managed. And broke into another round of sobs.

"Come and have some food. With me. And my wife. And my little girl. My leather shop is right there." He pointed across the road. "We are about to eat together. Join us."

I was confused. This man wasn't hitting on me (as I was used to). He was inviting me to join him and his family for dinner. Some crying stranger on the street. This would never happen in Singapore, I thought. "Okay. *Grazi. Grazi,*" I replied. I followed him into the store and the smell of fresh leather sobered me somewhat. Out the back of the store was a cute little courtyard, and his pretty pregnant wife sat playing with their three-year-old daughter. The table was laden with tomato pasta, sliced meats and cheeses and salad.

"I bring us a crying girl for dinner," the man said in broken English. I couldn't help but laugh. It was a little absurd.

"Hello. *Ciao! Mi chiamo,* Lena," I said.

"Lena, welcome," the woman said in perfect English. "Why are you crying? Please sit. Eat with us."

I awkwardly sat down. "I just arrived, and I felt all alone. And overwhelmed."

"A foreigner in a new city. Sometimes it happens," she responded. "I am Lucy, and this is my husband, Luigi. And this is our little girl, Charlotte." Charlotte skipped up to me and placed her doll on my lap. Her way of comforting a crying stranger.

There was something so beautiful about this moment. The kindness of strangers. To feel welcomed. Included. Cared for. I stayed for dinner. Luigi poured me a glass of the most delicious Chianti, and the warm homemade tomato pasta filled and comforted my belly.

I told them about the book I was writing and a little bit about being there to get over a broken heart. They listened. Validated. Offered me more wine and pasta. And told me I was welcome to join them for dinner anytime I felt lonely or overwhelmed. In their own way, they showed me love. After a helping of lemon slice and a tipple of limoncello, I said goodbye and wandered down the street to my apartment, my heart full.

I ran a bath and sat in it, letting a few more tears fall, before sleeping my first night in Florence. And when I woke in the morning, I was ready to write. I brewed some coffee on the stove, Italian style, and went out onto the balcony and wrote for a couple of hours.

My first two weeks in Italy were filled with magical moments like this. Welcoming the kindness of strangers. Crying into my coffee some mornings. Writing. Writing. Writing. And eating, eating, eating. Some evenings I had the urge to hop on the dating apps and see what kind of Italian hunks were around to entertain me, but I refrained. That itch was the itch of avoidance. And I was committed to feeling this grief. To stop running from it. And heal it. I wouldn't find men to soothe my pain anymore.

Instead of swiping, I'd sit in the bath, light a candle, cry and talk to myself. It might sound crazy, but for me, it was one of the most healing times of my life. Turning towards my heart and holding it so tenderly. And in no time at all, I had fifty thousand words of my book, a nurtured heart, and it was nearly time for Ellen to join me.

Ellen's arrival brightened my spirit on every level. We chatted into the night. We explored the boutiques in town. Hiked into the hills. Cooked together. And found some of the hidden top restaurants she'd been reading about online before her arrival. We shared stories about our mothers. The best sex of our lives. The worst sex of our lives. We listened to music and danced in the kitchen. It was a perfect girlfriend's getaway. As we were preparing pasta with prawns in the kitchen one evening, she looked up from chopping the spring onions and said "Girl, you are so amazing. I hope you really know that." And in that moment, I felt it. Like the love was inside my cells. That I was no longer alone in this world.

The Emptiness

When my mind

Is finally empty

I can feel the

Clenching

In my hips

The echo of my

Heartbeat

As it tells stories

Of worry

Fear

Aloneness.

And I can see

My mind trying

To fill itself up

Again

Making lists

Stories

Anything it can get

Its hands on

To distract me.

I ask my body

What it is afraid of

"The emptiness"

It replies.

So, I hold my

Beautiful

Timid body

In my awareness

Peering into the emptiness

Together

And my breath catches

Tears forming

In my throat.

That emptiness is endless

Like the ocean

That meets the certainty

Of the sky

So, I allow that

Horizon

To form

Inside myself

Where emptiness

And endlessness

Morph

Into each other

Become my breath

Become me

And in that moment

I become a little

Less afraid of myself.

My chest quivers

As a I let it all go

I settle into my own hips

Coming home

Even more

Than before

No longer empty

Endless.

Integration cannot be forced. It happens in its own time, often in the most unexpected and seemingly random moments.

I had returned from Italy a few weeks prior. It was nearly Christmas. Half of Singapore had left for holiday season, and I was enjoying the quiet to resettle into my rhythm, recover from jetlag and finish the final chapters of my book for the New Year's Eve deadline that was fast approaching.

The silky sunshine after the month in the crisp cold of early European winter was a daily gift. I'd spend time lying on the stone floor near my pool and sitting under the shaded umbrella with my computer and never-ending glasses of sparkling water with lime. A bikini and a damp towel were my uniform of choice.

Each day, I would rise, workout and perch myself in my favorite poolside spot to write for a few hours. And in the afternoons, I would play with my children, throw the ball in the pool, talk over dinner on the balcony. Dance with them to my daughter's favorite pop songs. Then I'd tuck them into bed with a full heart. The goodnight kiss on their little cheeks reverberating into my own cheeks and heart. After they would sleep, I'd often lay out my yoga mat, light some incense and enter a gentle meditation.

My body tended towards tightness. While I'd done so much work on clearing past trauma, it tended to brace, contract and tighten each day. It told stories of overload, emotion, and longing. And I had learned to listen to them as often as possible.

On December twenty-third, I completed the final chapter of my book. The kids and I celebrated mama's 'win' with grilled prawns, green noodles and mango salad by the pool. I treated myself to a glass of prosecco and they enjoyed a glass of sparkling apple cider. I let them stay up a little later and we snuggled onto the couch and watched an episode of my son's favorite manga tv show. I zoned out in bliss with one child on either side, my son's head on my shoulder and my daughter laying her head peacefully in my lap, her long pre-teen legs sprawled over the side of the sofa. I stroked her hair and took in the sense of connection and peace, here in my home, with my children. My son fell asleep towards the end of the episode, and I let him lay quietly in his slumber.

After it finished, I gestured to my daughter to brush her teeth and hair, and I carried my son into his bed and tucked him in. Next, I joined my daughter in her room and took over the task of brushing her long curls. Once I finished, I hugged her from behind and whispered, "I love you through the sky, past the sun, round the moon, and back into your heart." I could feel her smile. This was something I had been saying to them both since they were babies.

"I love you, too, Mama. So much. And I'm so proud of you for finishing your book." I felt her words right in my heart. Pure unconditional love.

"Thank you, baby. That's so special for me to hear. I hope you have dreams of rainbows and unicorns and all your favorite things." She giggled, hopped under the covers and reached her arms out for one more hug. I gave her a big squeeze, kissed her cheek and turned off the light.

I rolled out my yoga mat, set up my bolster lengthways and lay my back over it so I could open my heart. I folded my legs into a butterfly position and began to breathe. Into my heart. Into my hips. Feeling into areas of tension and then letting them release, dissolve, relax. I'd done this practice many times in recent months and often found myself sitting with a sense of emptiness that bridged through into an epic well of grief. But this time, as I sat with the emptiness inside my chest, it expanded into a deep blue ocean inside me. An endless ocean. The swell of its waves expanded inside me and my inner vision turned bright blue and then turquoise green.

My hips began to shake a little and my chest quivered as I let myself float in the vastness of this new feeling. Endlessness. Full of love. Full of possibility. I smiled in gratitude and a silent tear trickled down my left cheek. I felt present. Integrated. Like one chapter was closing and another beginning. I rolled onto my side and curled up. I lay there breathing, letting every single cell in my body know and learn this feeling. Endlessness.

My Poetry Partner

I was looking to be disrupted

Bored with the impressive

And delightful

Person I had become.

Itching to unleash

The wilderness

The epic garden

That had been growing

Inside me

And needed a bigger space

To flourish

And find

Its full brilliance.

I was too scared

To unzip myself

The lock to my glory

Could only be opened

By someone else.

And the door

To my secret garden

Would only ever budge

Even a little

In the safety

Of living dreams

Compartmentalized

From reality.

So, I sought you out

And asked if we could create

A container

For magic

Nice and neat.

Pretty and small.

But if I am honest

A part of me knew

Exactly what I was doing

Curating the stage

For my own emancipation.

I don't know if you saved me

Or destroyed me

But I knew it was

Exactly

What I had been looking for.

I don't think you knew

What your role

was meant to be

in my story

In fact

I think you were looking

For the exact same thing

A plot twist.

A disruption

A repatterning

A fucking fire

To blow your pain

To pieces

And reorder

Your world

In one way

or another.

And so, love

We gave that

To each other

An escape route

But damn

The other side

Is so lonely

Without you

My poetry partner.

And when I weep for you

I remind myself

That I am really

Weeping just for me

For what was lost

And for what has yet to come

These are my tears of creation

Thank you, love.

Routine and rhythm are a recipe for the road to success, but sometimes they are the enemy of creativity, magic and the delightful delirium of the unexpected.

Six months later, I had gotten in a great rhythm. Kids, work, self-care. It all was in flow. There was peace in my home, growth in my career. My manuscript was with my publisher, set to launch in eight month's time. I was feeling strong, fit and sleeping eight hours a night. But I was a little bored. I'd been off the dating apps and focusing on my own stability and happiness. And I was happy, if not a little restless. And I kept hurtling that restless energy towards my career. With great results.

My work was growing, as was my social media following. It felt like things were happening. Big things. Big impact. Big growth. My next US teaching trip was around the corner. New York, Ohio and LA, and this time I'd decided to visit Austin to meet some people from the world of therapy and healing.

I had been invited to stay with a friend who I'd met through the Singapore school mums grapevine which was lovely. I didn't know them very well but was touched to be invited to stay in their home on the outskirts of Austin, the brink of hill country.

Austin was my first stop before a hectic work trip. I had six days to get over the jetlag, see some live music and feel into the professional scene. And eat some darn good barbeque.

The city lit me up from the moment I set foot into the airport. The country vibe felt like music in my feet and sent some kind of creative expansive energy through my system. When I arrived at their house, Nellie welcomed me with open arms, poured me a glass of wine and took me out into their large garden, all kitted out with an outdoor bar and a hammock.

We chatted and realized we had so much in common, both spiritual seekers, with social hearts and a passion for seeding cultural change.

Austin seemed to be a mecca for people who were saying no to traditional ways of living and working. Entrepreneurs, artists and healers were sitting in cafes, strumming guitars and dreaming up a different way of doing life. I fit right in. I spent time meeting a people in my field, visiting healing spaces and imagining what it would be like to live there. From a professional point of view, there was amazing community available. Unfortunately, from a single mum point of view, it felt like it would be a hard slog, living on the outskirts of town, with a big house to manage and multiple school pick-ups and drop-offs every day. In so many ways, it was the opposite of my life in Singapore.

I'd been invited to attend a healing community event on Thursday afternoon. I was excited and a little nervous to sit amongst twenty peers. In all honesty, I wasn't used to being a peer anymore. I was used to being the teacher. The leader. The boss. The center of attention. And I knew that here, it would be a very different dynamic. The event commenced with the organizer sharing his intentions for the afternoon—bonding, sharing, play. Creativity. No selling. I liked the no selling bit. There is nothing worse than a room full of healers trying to sell to each other. So much ego, shadow and power struggle.

Upon the organizer's direction, we all packed our egos away neatly (or at least, tried to) and entered a sacred sharing circle. Most of the healers were relatively new in their careers. Either shyly sharing about their work, spilling out their own trauma stories or blurting out how they could heal every kind of illness under the sun because they'd figured out the keys to everything. I watched my judgmental mind come up as I listened to each share and gently replaced it with a compassionate and accepting energy. As best I could.

And then Dexter stood to speak, and the energy of the room totally changed. He had us all laughing hysterically while talking about his divorce, death and addiction. I was captivated by his presence and his ability to speak about such painful experiences with so much play and lightness. He was magic. Dexter was five foot seven, with a moderate build, a big great charming smile and a prominent nose. His chocolate brown hair was tucked behind his ears, and his dark brown eyes held so many stories. Wells of wisdom, pain and tenderness. I hadn't felt attracted to a man like this in a long time. Totally drawn in. Not to his physicality, but to his energy. His spirit.

After the sharing session, we broke for snacks and free time. Some people went out to the garden, while others gathered on the sofa to go deeper into conversation. A few picked up instruments that had been put out in another room. I stood sipping my peach flavored sparkling water, watching the scene before me. Orienting.

Dexter's voice spoke from behind me. "Peach is my favorite flavor." I turned around to see him standing there, smiling at me. "I am so darn drawn to you. Like a fucking magnet," he said boldly.

I smiled at his directness. "I'm drawn to you, too, Dexter. I love the way you brought humor to the group today. I'm Lena, by the way."

"I know who you are, Lena. Your reputation precedes you." He smiled.

I felt myself blushing. He sure knew how to stroke my ego.

He fidgeted a little. "Look, I need to go and collect my daughter from school now. But I want to know you. I need to know you. I'm flying off the day after tomorrow for a shoot. Are you free to come visit my place in hill country tomorrow? We can drink more peach soda, sit in my yard, talk."

"I'll be there. Send me a pin."

There was an undeniable electric current in the air between us. A sizzle. That was far more than sexual. It was spiritual. That's how it felt. We exchanged numbers and he stepped forward and hugged me goodbye. He lingered a little and whispered in my ear, "See you tomorrow."

Arriving at Dexter's hill country home felt like a scene from a movie. We'd agreed to meet at noon. The uber drove me through the expansive rolling hills and the sun shone above like some kind of big 'yes girl' signal, encouraging me all the way. I was wearing black yoga pants with a bit of a sheen to them, a white cotton halter top with a bare back and my favorite green and white kimono. My wrists jangled with their usual gold bangles, and my hair was pulled back with a silk hair scarf, revealing gold hoop earrings. My make up was 'barely there' giving me a 'this girl is a natural summer beauty' vibe. On my feet I had some simple gold leather flip flops to complete the look.

Dexter was waiting for me in his driveway, cowboy hat and all, holding two cans of peach soda with a giant grin on his face. "Hey, girl, hey! You made it," he greeted me. As I walked towards him, he placed the cans on the ground and leapt forward and embraced me in a big bear hug and gave me a kiss on the cheek. "Welcome to hill country. We are lucky to have you here." I blushed a little and a sizzle moved up the back of my spine.

Dexter showed me the house and the epic grounds, including a giant yard full of wildflowers, complete with a swing set and trampoline for his kids, a wooden sauna, ice bath and meditation 'cave' as well as his top floor recording studio. Even if I wasn't already attracted to this charismatic creature, this place was enough to make any girl instantly wet.

"I thought we could eat a chopped chicken salad, drink some peach soda and dive deep into each other's souls. Sound good?" He laughed out loud. He had the kind of deliciously free laugh that would always invite those listening to join him.

"Love it," I said. "Let's do it."

We sat on his porch with big helpings of salad in wide flat pottery bowls and our sodas. Dexter gave me the short version of his life. He was newly separated with four kids ranging from seven to seventeen years old. It was emotional. Messy. Unclear. But it was happening. He was also supporting himself in this glorious set up while his kids and his ex who were living in the same suburb as my girlfriend on the outskirts of Austin. He made his living as a coach and an influencer, as well as holding some men's groups and psychedelic journeys in his home.

But at heart, he told me, he was a musician and a poet. He'd also been exploring his sexuality. Reading everything he could get his hands on about it and practicing a certain type of yoga to feel more embodied and present with his masculinity. And on top of that, he had quit drinking and caffeine and not masturbated in sixty days. It sounded like a lot.

He told his story with the same kind of humor as he had during the group event the day before. I sat there, laughing and honestly wowed by how much charisma he had, and how dedicated he seemed to be to his healing, amidst all he was navigating. I was impressed. And I was turned on.

After I reciprocated with my mini 'let's get to know each other' bio he said, "You are so fucking hot. I'm so attracted to you. I don't know if that's okay to say, but I'm saying it."

"You can say it," I replied, almost daring him to make his next move.

He had been sitting opposite me and got up and joined me on the long porch sofa where I was sitting. I could feel his breath, his pulse, his heartbeat. He spoke slowly. "I've never felt so attracted to anyone. Ever."

Music to any female ego's ears. I was his. It wasn't about my ego. Something about Dexter felt exciting. Creative. Disruptive. My attraction to him came from a part of me that was bored and wanted to play. A part of me that was feeling restless and unsatisfied with the consistent calm I had begun to cultivate in my life. In the moment, I filed him under 'cute travel romance'. "Why don't you try kissing me first and see how that goes, cowboy?" I replied.

"Yes, Ma'am." He played along, took off his cowboy hat, leaned in and kissed me. He kissed like a rockstar. The perfect amount of lips, tongue and lingering between movements, sending sparkles through my cells. After a few minutes of gentle kissing, we came up for air and he said, "You know the hat is only for show right? I'm no cowboy."

I didn't reply. Instead, I pulled him on top of me and placed his hand on my ass. "Today, you're a cowboy," I joked.

"Mmm hmmm," he murmured and buried his head in the side of my neck while his hand explored my yoga pant-clad ass. We kissed and petted for a while and then he said, "Let me make us a nest. Give me two minutes."

He grabbed a picnic rug and a few cushions and set up a little makeshift make out pad for us, in his yard, under the Texan sun. He lay down and unbuttoned his shirt.

"What now, Ma'am?" he asked. I was still sitting on the sofa on the porch.

This is just like a movie, I thought. So why not play into it? A micro-moment of shame passed through my body. "Don't be a slut, Lena," it whispered. I set a swift boundary with it and told myself, *I am an empowered sexual creature and single as can be. I can do what I like.* And with that, I stood up and slowly removed my kimono and yoga pants, turned around and showed him my back. I untied the slim white string of my halter top and removed it. All that was left was a hot pink G-string. "Shall I come over there?" I smiled at him.

Dexter gulped. I could tell he felt a little out of his depth. I quite liked the feeling of being 'the experienced one', the woman with the sexual prowess who was going to show this innocent cowboy how it was done. I strode over the picnic rug and lay down next to him. We lay silently for a few minutes, just taking each other in. Then he gasped, "Holy moly, girl. I am the luckiest cowboy," and moved towards me.

We kissed and fondled for hours. He didn't approach my panties at all. But he roamed my neck, breasts and back. While I had been leading at first, the roles had switched naturally, as I could see he needed space to tune in, feel and find his way. While on the one hand it was incredibly sexual, it also felt rather pure. Like watching a young foal learning to gallop for the first time.

Some hours into our playtime, the sky began to turn a beautiful orange. Sunset was upon us. I had plans for dinner, so I needed to wrap up. And while I wanted to continue laying and playing with him there on the rug, I also thought it was kind of nice that we hadn't actually had sex. Especially as I likely wouldn't see him again. "I better get back. The sun's setting and my friend's expecting me for dinner with her family," I said.

"I get it. Let me drive you back, but on the way, I want to show you the sunset from my favorite spot."

We got dressed and he took my hand and led me to his sleek black convertible. As we drove, he steered with one hand and used his free one to grasp mine. He'd put on a playlist of cool country tunes that were so Texas, I had to smile. And he sang along to them as we drove through hill country, up to a high peak where he pulled over in an empty field for us to watch the sun go down with the top down. It felt like utter magic. The orangey pink sun setting over the hills. The music. The man singing with his coarse, crooning voice. His hand in mine.

This can't be the end, I thought to myself.

Just then, he looked over at me and said, "I want to know you forever. You're in me now. And I'm in you. Just remember that."

I was lost for words and just nodded, my eyes welling with tears of longing. Tears of leaving. Tears.

He dropped me back at my friend's and got out of the car to kiss me goodbye. He kissed me deeply. With so much intention. "Keep in touch, girl," he said, his tone now casual, a mismatch from the intensity of our time together. "You know I'm in the depths of it all right now. Divorce. Kids. Healing myself. I have no idea what's going to happen. But I'm fucking glad I met you. You're one hell of a woman."

I didn't know how to respond. So, I said, "Take care, Dexter," turned and went inside.

I knew the encounter was likely a one-off incredibly connected experience. Yet I couldn't stop thinking about him. Replaying the scene in my mind again and again. It felt like living poetry. Art. It had felt like the kind of movie I had imagined for myself, yet never found myself in.

And just as I had begun to accept I wouldn't hear from Dexter again… ping… there it was, a voice message. Dexter explained he had been busy with divorce stuff, kids' stuff and work stuff, but had been thinking of me daily. Along with the message, he sent a few pictures. Him. His daughter all dressed up for a school event. A sunset.

And so, our little voice message exchange began. A quasi relationship built on voice messages and a few images once a week or so. While I continued to live on, I couldn't get Dexter out of my head. He'd sparked new life in me. New hunger. A kind of creative energy. An excitement. And before I knew it, it was time for me to plan my next work trip. There was no reason for me to go to Austin. I had a job in New York and then one in the Netherlands after that. But Austin wasn't too much of a detour. And I wanted to feel more of what I had felt with Dexter. The poetry of it all. The playfulness of it.

So, I put it out there. "How do you feel about me coming to spend some one-on-one time with you. Maybe four days or so?"

After I sent the message, my anxiety spiked. Fear of rejection. And I immediately wished I hadn't sent it. But after three days of cringing, waiting and hoping, Dexter replied, "I'm in. Let's do this. I can't wait to see you in six weeks."

We began planning a four-day deep dive: Dex and Lena do hill country. We decided I would stay at his home, and we would drop into some sacred time together. We had a call to discuss expectations and boundaries. He clearly told me, "I want to be clear. I am not relationship-able. But I want you. There's potential magic here." Unconsciously, I chose not to process the first sentence. I focused on the notion that he wanted me.

Potential magic. I wanted that. No matter what came along with it.

Souls And Bones

I could feel you

Underneath it all

Your perfect misshapen soul

And I knew

You could feel mine too

Underneath the junk

Of our humanness.

I wanted to jump

Out of my body

And meet you

In some field

With long grass

And wildflowers

Eternal sunshine

Where music emitted

From our heartbeats

And fingers

Where together we were

Living poetry.

I knew that my feet

Could take me there

That I could grow

A pair of wings

And fly into the fantasy

And all the while

Keep my feet on the ground

In the mainstream dimensions.

But I also knew

That you couldn't

At least not now

Not yet

There was no structure

Holding your world in place

No farmers or family

Tending to you

So you had to stay

And sort it out

And even though

I understood

The earthly realities

I stamped my foot a little

I wanted to take you away

From it all

And play.

Instead,

I sent you

Safety and hope

From my bones to yours

A sacred transmission.

I raked my zen garden

And flew into some other

Fantastic reverie

Hoping you'd find

Your own sweet way

To meet me there.

A profound connection is somewhat meaningless when there is no structure to hold it. When there are not two hearts and four hands that are willing to mold it.

The connection I had with Dexter was unlike any I had experienced before. We woke something in each other. Stirred something in each other.

He was waiting for me at the Austin airport standing in front of the giant guitar at baggage claim with his ridiculous heartwarming smile, his ripped jeans and his pink floral shirt. No hat this time. I spotted him before he spotted me, and my heart skipped a beat. As soon as he saw me, he ran forward and took me in his arms. After a warm hug that spoke a thousand words, he pulled back and held my shoulders and said, "I am so glad you're here. I'm excited for us to be sweet to each other." My heart melted a little.

He took my large suitcase, and we headed towards his car for the drive to his home. I could tell he was nervous as he parked my suitcase in his bedroom. He paused and turned to me, "Do you want to sleep in the same bed as me?"

"Of course I do," I smiled. "I can't wait to lay my head on your pillow."

He seemed relieved. "Are you hungry? Do you want a soda? Do you want to go for a walk? What do you feel like?" he inquired, eager to please.

"Actually, I would like some porch time with you," I said. He led me to the porch and chose to sit on a separate sofa than me. "Are you a bit nervous?"

"Mmmm, not really," he lied. "Actually, yeah. I don't know what I'm doing or what to expect or if I can even be a nice guy for a whole four days. I was a shithead to my wife. So, I'm trying something new with you. And I don't know if I'm going to be able to be a nice guy. I want to be a nice guy."

"You are a nice guy," I said. "A really nice guy."

At the time, I was enamored with what seemed to be a genuine desire to connect and care for me but was really a declaration of his inability to sustain such behavior and a tendency to revert into a carless lover, partner or whatever role he was trying on in our little experiment.

I got up off my sofa and moved over to share his. I sat close to him. Silently. And we just looked at each other.

"Hi," he said with a goofy smile.

"Hi," I returned the greeting, and we both giggled.

He picked up the guitar that was resting on the side of the sofa. He played and sung. An original song. It was all about wanting a woman from afar. I could tell he'd written it for me. As he reached for the high notes, my heart opened, and my pants were wet with lust. Such. A. Turn on.

When he finished, he put the guitar down and said, "That was about you."

I nodded and jumped him. After getting naked and spending some time kissing and stroking each others' bodies, fooling around on the outdoor sofa, he took my hand and led me into his bedroom. He paused, and I realized I was likely the first woman he had brought in here since his split.

"This is big for me," he said, confirming my thoughts. "I'm so pleased that this is happening with you. It was meant to be you."

He had this way of saying words that bypassed any of my pessimistic self-protective tendencies and had me opening my heart and my legs in nanoseconds. But this time, there was a gentleness to it. A tenderness. An innocence. I let him explore my body like it was a foreign land. I let him seek out my clitoris and gave him clues like he was on a treasure hunt. He did very well at following them.

One hour and three orgasms later, he went to enter me. I told him he needed to wear a condom, and he repelled a bit. "I've never worn a condom before. I don't even have any."

I tried to hide my shock. "Well, if you want to be inside me, you need to wear one. I've got some in my suitcase." I sprung up and flung a few on the bedside table. I passed him one. He looked concerned. "Let me," I offered and proceeded to cover his cock with protective plastic.

A little bit about Dexter's cock. It was clearly inexperienced. It was clearly a little smaller than I'd like. But I loved it. Because it was his.

He rolled me over and mounted me. But he'd gone flaccid. And he was clearly embarrassed. He tried to joke it off.

"Hey," I interjected. "It's ok. Just lay with me. Kiss me. There is no pressure. No rush. Lay with me."

He rolled off and curled next to me and buried his head in my breasts. He lay there for some time, nuzzling me, while I stroked his back. After a while, I could feel him becoming aroused again. He started kissing me with fervor. Pressing his body against me, thrusting. He placed his semi-hard cock between my thighs but didn't dare enter. He started breathing rhythmically and asked me to breathe with him. So, I did. He then started telling me what he was doing with his 'energetic dick.'

"Up through your yoni, to your belly. Can you feel me there? I'm in your belly."

Weirdly (or not so weirdly) I could. And it felt fucking amazing. He continued to tell me where he was placing his energetic dick while his real live one probed around between my thighs, tantalizing my dripping pussy.

Up to my heart. Into my throat. Into my third eye. Through my entire center. Dexter was doing energy work with his not so worldly dick. His energy dick. I'd never experienced anything like it. And as I yielded into the energetic deliciousness of it all, I had a micro-pause of fear. Could he scramble up my psyche with his powerful energy dick? I decided to let go of fear and simply trust.

"I always wondered if I could do energy work with my dick. I've dreamed of doing this. And I fucking love, Lena, that you're so, so sensitive and responsive to it."

"You're a sex wizard," I complimented him and watched his fragile ego grow as he received it. And his dick too. He quickly entered me, thrust about for a few minutes and then came. As he came, he cried.

"I'm grateful for you, so grateful," he murmured as he kissed me all over my face.

I didn't know what to make of it. While I was deeply touched by his sensitivity, I was also aware that I was about five orgasms underserved. I was quite a tiger between the sheets with lots of energy to tussle and thump and ride my man, but it was clear Dexter was done for the evening.

"Let me spoon you to sleep," he suggested. And I obediently rolled over and let him continue to enjoy the experience his way.

Surprisingly, I slept well. I felt very safe in Dexter's energy. And so comfortable and peaceful in his hill country home. When I opened my eyes, he was laying opposite me, gazing at me. "I love your face on my pillow, Chica. Good morning." It was such a beautiful way to wake up.

"Good morning." I rolled into him and kissed his chest, then sprung out of bed. "Let me pee. I'll be right back."

I dashed, naked, into the ensuite, relieved my bladder and gave my teeth a quick brush, and joojed my messy bed hair. I returned to the bedroom and slid into bed, keeping a little distance from him. We looked at each other for a while. Then he gently took my resting hand and placed it on his hard, ready dick. I took it as a cue to climb on top of him. My hair fell like a golden curtain around his face, and we were back in our sexual energy tent.

"You're fucking beautiful. I'm taking a snapshot in my head right now."

I smiled, dripping with desire. "Do you want to put a condom on?" I enquired.

"No," he replied. "I don't like them, I've decided. I'm clean. We don't need one."

I immediately contracted. "Sorry, this is a boundary for me. And it's not only about STDs. It's about fertility. Respect. Safety on so many levels."

"I hear you," he validated. "I don't want to do anything you don't want me to. So, let's fool around this morning, no sex. Plus, I want to take my girl to a fancy breakfast."

Again, I didn't know what to make of the moment, the subtle power play that was going on. And found myself, for a second time in only a few hours, sexually unfulfilled. But I didn't say anything, I just went with the energy of the moment, and we lay and kissed and rubbed up against each other for another half an hour, until my tummy started rumbling. I took it as a cue to transition towards breakfast.

I took a shower and put on a cute floral two-piece shirt and shorts set. I kept my bedhead and added a bit of extra volume and chose to keep it light and lovely with some tinted moisturizer, bronzer, and a lick of pink lip-gloss. I walked out into the open plan living and dining area, and Dexter was waiting for me with coffee. "You're gorgeous," he offered. "I made you a to-go coffee with maple syrup to keep you going. I'm taking you for the best breakfast in Austin. You ready?"

I stepped forward and kissed him lightly. "Mmmhmmm," I said.

We drove to a cute breakfast spot near South Congress and sat and ate and chatted. Well, he chatted. And I listened. He told me about his marriage, the split, his four kids and his dreams of growing a kind of spiritual church where men and families could heal and commune together. It sounded beautiful. Inspirational. I was so struck by his spiritual vision, I didn't take time to question the details about how he was going to build it.

After breakfast, he said, "I want to treat you. A woman like you needs a great set of cowboy boots. To dance the earth in."

He took me to a large cowboy boot store. Rows and rows of colored boots. High ones, low ones. Leather or suede. Patterned or plain. I went to the section that had my size, and as I tried on each pair, I twirled and posed for him to see. My 'Pretty Woman' moment. I settled on a pair of light turquoise suede boots. They were perfect for me. I kissed his cheek to thank him for the gift.

"You'll remember me always, Chica. Every time you wear your boots. Doesn't matter that I don't know how I am going to pay my rent," he laughed.

I winced at the rent remark. Memories of my mother glided through my mind. She used to love to take me shopping, treat me, make me feel like a princess. Then there would be the inevitable shame and blame. "You're bleeding me dry, Lena. You're making me broke, you selfish girl." I shook off the memories and reminded myself he's not my mother and simply said, "Thank you, Dex, I love them."

We spent the next two days listening to music, writing poetry together, kissing, fondling and bonding at a very deep level. On the last day, my period came. And I felt a little achy and low, as I always do. He was very caring, rubbing my back, getting me pillows and tea. Care has always been my favorite love language, and he was showing it to me in spades. Noticing this, I felt teary. The end of our time together was coming. It had been so beautiful; I didn't want it to end. I let my tears fall, deciding not to hide my tender heart from him. Initially he looked a little alarmed.

Dexter had told me stories about having to self-abandon to constantly meet his ex-wife's emotional needs, so I knew what was coming up for him.

"Hey, you don't need to make my tears go away, Dex. They are tears of gratitude. And I'm sharing them with you. I've had the most beautiful time with you. There's no burden here, okay?"

As he let the words sink in, I could tell there was a new relational template forming inside him. Where feminine emotional expression was not a threat to his existence. "You're amazing. This time with you has been, still is, life changing. I know that nothing is going to be the same again."

That night, as we lay in bed, playing our sexual energy games, I wanted him so badly. He, again, refused my request to wear a condom, and through a mixture of deep yearning, sexual frustration and the knowing that my bleed would ensure I would not get pregnant, I thrust myself down on his cock and rode him quietly, slowly, lovingly. I breeched my hard and fast rule—no glove, no love. Because then and there, the love seemed more important.

The next day, Dexter drove me to the airport and we both had tears in our eyes the whole way. "You have no idea how good this is. I wish you had more dating experience to compare it to," I said.

"I do know how good this is. You are the real deal. But I need time. To date. To be single. To fuck around. I have a feeling I'm not going to like what I find, but it's something I have to go through."

"I do. I have a feeling you need a couple of years for that."

"We are not over, Chica," he said. "You know that, right?"

I nodded, holding back a flood of tears. I had known coming into our time together, which he labelled as a 'portal,' he was not ready for a relationship of any kind. Plus, I lived on the other side of the world. Everything about his world was unstable. Mid-divorce, learning how to be a single dad to four young kids, figuring out how to pay the bills. There was no way he could give me the long-term love I really wanted. I knew it rationally. But my heart still yearned for this man.

As we pulled up at the airport drop-off zone, I said, "I wish you so much peace. Liberation. And Love. All the love."

"Chica..." he said, lost for words. He took my suitcase out of the trunk, and we embraced one last time. He kissed the tears rolling down my cheeks and said, "You'll hear from me. This is not our ending. I just have some stuff to figure out."

I nodded, kissed him one more time, and turned to enter the airport terminal.

And I sat there at the gate, letting the tears fall. Tears that spoke of all the love that could not be realized at this time.

The Cliffs Of You

Dangling on the cliff

Of your unconscious

Feeling the long drop

To the ground

And your fearful finger

Poised to push me off

I clung there for a while

Grabbing at you

As gently as I could

Then I realized

The torture of holding on

Was far greater

Than the fall below

So I let go

And found myself

Crumpled on the ground.

I cried like a little baby

I cried like a woman who

Lost her greatest love

I cried like a mermaid

Stranded on a rock

In some strange sea

The enormity of it made

No sense.

I cried from all my parts

Because they had all been dancing

With you

And not one of them could fathom

Not being with you again

So I cried

And held myself in my mess

I waited briefly

For you to meet me in this

Complex devastation

But I soon knew

You would not come

Because you were too busy

Licking your wounds

And wrestling with your own monster

Occupied.

So I threw a penny in the lake of

Love lost

I wished you liberation, love and peace

Then I let you go

And walked home to myself once more

Shanti shanti shanti

Immature hearts will often grow hands that cannot hold others. Uncontained hearts will often grow tentacles that pull people into their mess. Reckless hearts grow hands that will grab and discard when and as they wish.

What had begun as a beautifully, sacred container with Dexter, turned into a long-distance game of torture. After I left, holding my tender and heart and all the grief of what could not be, I felt proud of the level of maturity I had reached on my journey of love. I let the exchange be what it was and not to force or grow it into anything more. I had learned to love and let go, or so I thought.

It was Dexter who reached out, his confused heart spilling all over the place. I received message after message of him sharing how much I'd touched his heart. A mix of voice notes, texts and links to songs on Spotify that expressed his feelings. I tried to hold back from engaging too much, but then he sent a message that broke the energetic damn that I had built between our long-distance hearts.

It said, "Lena, it honestly feels like if I died right now, I'd be happy... because the things I experienced with you, I never knew were possible. Your moans. Your scent. Your receptivity. Your abandon. In fact, it would kind of be easier to die than to navigate the future. Love you, Chica."

As I listened to the intense expression of his heart, I lost all sense of reality. I wanted to be with Dexter. And I was willing to move mountains to make it happen. We started texting or voice-noting regularly. Long messages about our days. Short, sweet messages of love and care. We exchanged songs each day. Because of the time difference, he became the first person I communicated with in the morning, as I was the last he spoke to before sleep. And I'd dream of him most nights. The haze of eros was upon me. Dexter, Dexter, Dexter. Everything Dexter.

We scheduled a video call to check in and connect face-to-face. He opened the call by telling me he missed me.

"I can be back in Texas in about eight weeks. I have six weeks free, and I was going to go to Europe to write my next book. But I could come and be with you. We could try this out. I need to be in the US after that anyway for work."

He was silent for a moment and closed his eyes. "That feels like a lot of pressure. I don't know if I can handle a week of being the kind of guy you deserve."

"I don't want it to feel like a pressure," I replied. "But we've both been saying we miss each other and want each other, and I'm saying, 'Hey Dex, I can make this happen. I'll rearrange my schedule. I'll hop on a plane. I'm aware that you don't have as much stability or freedom in your life as I do, so I'm trying to make it possible... to dip in... to explore.'"

"I hear you. And I fucking love that. But I am not ready for long term commitment."

"I know, and I'm not asking for that. I am also not ready either. It will take me a year or two of dating to really know if I want to commit. I'm talking about six weeks, to try it out."

"Lena," he replied. "You know I love you, Chica, but I'm going to need some space to think about this."

"How much space?" I asked, feeling my heart sink and the bubbles of the anxiety that were to take over my world while he took some space to think about my offer.

"Give me a week. Let me feel into it. Then we can have another video call and get clear together."

"Okay," I agreed. "Should we still send voice messages and texts, or not?"

"I think... not. Real space. I need to feel myself."

"Alright. Let's take some space. I definitely want you to lean in or out from an honest space."

"That's what I fucking love about you. The real deal. That's you. Alright. I'll see you." And with that, the phone call ended. And I entered a week of total purgatory.

The anxiety. The grief. The anger that came up was like an eruption of my inner volcano. I was climbing the walls. Processing. Crying. Writing. Longing. Purging. And most importantly, holding back from reaching out, projecting anything on to him. Sticking to our agreement. Giving him space to choose.

And while a part of me thought I was offering him his sovereignty and healing my past tendency to lure unavailable men into my field, there was another part of me that knew I had totally given up my power and placed myself in his rotten waiting room.

During that week my skin broke out. I had welt like pimples on my chin and forehead. My feet became tense and sore, and my stomach was in knots. I couldn't eat or sleep. The starkness of going from being intertwined in each other's energy to not feeling his presence at all felt like torture. Like I was detoxing off the sweetest addiction.

"You know what I am going to say," said Ellen. After five days that seemed like five months, I sat with her and Charlie in my living room, looking like a ghost of myself.

"He's not your guy," I whispered. "I know. I see that."

I felt frustrated with the familiarity of this scene. The distressed, disempowered woman sitting crying over an unavailable man with my besties trying to comfort me. Hadn't I learned my lesson with Lucas? What on earth was wrong with me that I kept finding myself back here? At least I had the awareness to see the pattern. My own disdain didn't soothe my spirit at all.

"It is so not cool for him to demand total silence. What's that about? You offered to fly halfway across the world to try it out and he's acting like you're a burden. What a gift you offered him. You didn't ask for marriage. Or commitment. And if he's triggered by that, then he really isn't going to be able to handle you. And let's be honest, this guy is in the middle of a messy divorce, has six mouths to feed and an unstable financial world. He's never going to be able to give you what you want, what you deserve. I know you felt amazing with him, but a few days of passion do not indicate if someone can really show up and love you. He can't, honey," reasoned Ellen.

"You're right," I whispered and took a sip of tea which I barely swallowed before bursting into tears.

"Aw, babe," sympathized Charlie. "I hear what you're saying, Ellen, but maybe space is good. Maybe he'll realize how amazing Lena is and invite her into his world. There is something big for men around invitations and power dynamics. He might be overwhelmed. In situations like this where there's clearly triggers going on, I'm all for information gathering and letting things play out. I think that your heart totally opened with Dexter. I've never seen you so soft, vulnerable and open to love. Really open. And so, stuff is coming up. This space isn't just for him, you know. It's for you too."

"I get it. My heart really does feel open," I said, and another surge of tears emerged.

Both women held important yet opposing viewpoints. I needed to move through this time and get back on the phone, face-to-face and feel him. But in my heart, if I was honest, at that moment, I knew it needed to be over. He would never be able to meet me. However, part of my heart held hope that his desire for me would outweigh the practicality of his situation and have him find a way to love me, just for a while. These were the delusions of my heart that yearned so deeply for this man... or at least, for the projection of him I had created.

For the last few days of the agreed silence, I had dreams of Dexter fucking another woman. A small American girl with dirty blonde knotty hair. They were upsetting. And I told myself that this was more delusion. And that even if it wasn't, he had every right to be with anyone he wanted. We were not in a committed relationship.

By the day we were supposed to reconnect, I had come to the decision I couldn't do this dance with him. That it wasn't good for my mental health. My physical health. And it was taking me away from feeling the general balance, joy and direction that had become such a big part of my daily life. I waited patiently for him to reach out. But the silence remained. For two more days. And instead of the longing and grieving I had been bathing in, I found myself transitioning to feelings of rage. This felt disrespectful. Hurtful. Mean. This did not feel okay. So, I decided to shift the energy of it all by reaching out.

Thinking of you. Are you ready to have that video call?

After I sent the message, I waited with bated breath for his reply. Nearly twenty-four hours went past and after a fitful sleep with more dreams of him and 'Miss America,' I woke the next morning to a short text that said, *Soon, Chica.*

What the hell did that mean?! It felt like I was being plunged back into his waiting room, with no clarity, only confusion. As though I was dangling on the cliffs of his world, waiting for him to either help me up or push me into the vast ocean below. Anguish. Then rage. More rage. Another fitful sleep. And then the next morning, I woke to his invitation for a video call.

Chica, Let's chat.

It was early morning my time on a Saturday. My children were sleeping in their beds. I'd set my alarm early to prepare and center for a six am call. It was mid-afternoon in Texas. I brewed some coffee, thew on a kimono, brushed my hair and added a lick of lip-gloss. I meditated myself into a false sense of centeredness. It was the only thing I could do. While I had all kinds of thoughts and feelings about our dynamic, I wanted to listen first and hear where he was at.

"I always forget how beautiful you are," he began the call. "It's so good to see you. To feel you."

I sighed, adopting the softness that his compliments tended to bring out in me. "Hi, Dex."

"I want to get funky with you, Lena. Super honest. So, I'm gonna share where I am at. And when I'm done, you can tell me how you feel. M'kay? I'm fucking attracted to you. You're a life changing woman. And I want to lean in with you. I want to date you. I want you here in Austin, but not because of me. Fuck, I don't even know how I am going to feel tomorrow, let alone in two months. So, come. Great. Awesome. Be in Austin. And I'll see if I'm open to dating you a bit when you're here. But I can't promise you anything. I don't want that kind of responsibility right now. I'm trying on the asshole costume.

I know I am, and you know what? It doesn't feel good, but I need to put myself first. I don't want to lose myself. And it would be so easy to get lost in a woman like you. You're like a beautiful ocean I want to swim in forever. And I don't want to be in an ocean right now, you know? I need to date a bunch of women and get some experience, and I have a feeling I'm not going to like what I find out there, but I gotta do it."

He paused. And I digested in silence. This was exactly what he had told me last time we were together. He hadn't changed. But thank fuck, I had. The week of silence had sobered me.

"One more thing," he added. "I'm exploring another connection too. A girl I met at LAX airport. She knows all about you. I told her how much I like you and how connected we are and that we are building something. And she's cool with it. She's chill. I guess I want to be honest, 'cause you know, that could grow, too. I don't know if it will, but it could."

"You were with her this last week, weren't you? I could feel it. I dreamed about it."

"Yeah, you're super fucking connected. You knew. Of course you knew," he affirmed. "So that's where I am at. I want to date you. Come to Austin. Let's see what happens."

My response shocked me, but it felt honest in my bones. "I am too good for this. You cannot have me like this."

"Oh man, I like you even more for setting a boundary," he replied and laughed a little.

I was repulsed by the humor he found in my rejection of his idea. "You honestly think it would be appropriate for me to put energy into coming to Austin, leaving my kids, giving up my Europe writing trip, to come and sit in your stinking hot summer in an apartment alone, just hoping you'll take me on a few dates? If that is the kind of woman you want, I am not for you. And that girl you've been fucking all week? She clearly has no standards or boundaries to lay next to you while you tell her how much you 'dig' me. She can fucking have you. I'm out, Dexter. I'm out."

My cheeks were hot with anger and tears pricked the corners of my eyes.

"I can feel your fire, Chica," he replied and put his hand on his heart. "I respect that this is not how you want to be in relationship, but that's all I've got for you right now."

I took a grounding breath. I was determined not to turn him into a perpetrator. I reminded myself I knew exactly what stage of life he was in when I met him. But I was also sure as hell that I could not engage on his ridiculous and disrespectful terms. "Dexter, I knew it was over before our call. I know you cannot love me the way I deserve to be loved right now. And I want to wish you so much love, so much peace, so much of everything that you wish for. And yeah... I guess that's it. I had the most magical time with you these last months. You touched my heart. And it opened so wide for you. So wide. And I suppose, now I need to figure out what to do with it all. Without you."

"Chica... I... I...," Dexter began. He wanted to lean back into the fantasy that we were exiting. "Let's talk again in a few weeks?"

"I'm not sure," I replied. "I need to get on with my life. Plan my travels. Reorient my heart. Now it's me who needs space. Because two things are clear: I don't want to date you. Not like this. And I'm not coming to Austin."

"Got it," he said. "You're in my heart forever. Nothing will ever be the same after you. Just know that."

Part of me wanted to rescind my words and hop on a plane and into his avoidant messed up arms. But a stronger part of me wanted to throw up in my mouth a little. But both parts, when I sat with them, took me to my heart, which felt totally broken. Shattered, in fact. But around my shattered heart was a halo of trust that was forming, letting me know that I was learning to keep myself safe. A discerning heart is a safe heart. So, I sat with my heart, shattered, yet safe.

Little Gifts In The Sand

These men

Who get under

My skin

And then rip it off

My body.

They're both

Fucking me up

And reminding me

Just how much

Light I hold

Just how much

Power resides

In the wells

Of my spirit.

And after

Each one of them

Is gone

I rise up

Eventually

Glorious

A phoenix returned.

My heart

Richer

My bones

Wiser

My mind

Humbled

My wits

Sharpened.

And I walk on

With my lessons

And my stories

Spinning in the field

Around me.

My footprints

Little gifts in the sand

For fellow travelers

As I journey on

To the next adventure

Our capacity to grieve and release what is not meant for us often opens the doorway to what is. As I let Dexter go, my creative energy reawakened. I was pouring it into my writing. At the same time, the stable ground that had been beneath my feet for so many years in Singapore split wide open. At one point, it felt like I was being swallowed, but then, I realized I had energetic wings and could fly to find and land on new ground.

One Monday morning, I got a text from Joseph that said, *We need to talk. Are you free to chat?* I knew this could not be good. Joseph never communicated with such starkness or urgency. It wasn't his way unless there was a problem.

On the phone, he told me he had been made redundant and had thirty days to leave Singapore. And that he wanted to take our children with him back home to Sydney, as well as his long-term girlfriend and her child. It was a lot to swallow, and I could feel my mind swirling with all kinds of reactive replies, which I had enough wisdom to hold back. I let him know I needed some time to digest.

I sat with it. I talked to my girlfriends. And to Tabitha. Thank goodness for Tabitha. The truth of the matter was, I had become quite global in the last few years. I was often on a plane to the United States and had been feeling pulled to start working and travelling in Europe. Singapore wasn't lighting me up anymore. Every time I returned home from a trip, I experienced a mini depression of sorts and felt quite empty. When travelling, I felt alive and inspired. I really felt like a fish out of water in Singapore. Or like a butterfly that didn't have space to flap her wings. I had begun to feel compressed and lonely there. But Australia really wasn't somewhere I wanted to be. I had never been happy there. There were so many traumatic memories there. And it was so darn far from everywhere else.

I had the power to decide on the fate of the family. After co-parenting peacefully in sunny Singapore for seven years, everything was going to change. Drastically. Our court order stated that neither parent could take the children out of the country without consent from the other. Joseph's ability to take the children with him rested entirely in my hands. After many conversations with all the various people in my life, he and I came to an agreement. I'd consent to the children going to Australia with him, if he chose a home within a walk of my father's home and my sister's home. So that the children would have a village. He'd take on the role of primary carer for one to two years and I would take my time to navigate my next move, not only feeling into Australia, but exploring my international footprint with more freedom. It was a highly untraditional arrangement. But there was little to nothing that was traditional about my life to begin with.

A couple of months later, we all found ourselves back in Sydney. To my surprise and delight, the kids immediately took to their homeland. They loved spending time with their family and slid right into school life, each making a few friends within the first few weeks. I was coming and going from Sydney back to Singapore, where my business was, and the United States where I was teaching. There were six months of intense travel. Running an international business. Flights. Hotel rooms. So many time zones. Jetlag. There was also expansion. Creativity. A horizon of possibility.

I'd been reading some of my new poetry to Esther and she suggested I try to do something with it. She linked me up to a university, and within a few weeks 'The Living Poetry Project' was born. She was somewhat of a magician, that woman. A visionary who knew how to make things happen. A rare combination.

The project sat at the intersection of the arts and social impact. I worked with a small group of students and used my poetry to inspire conversations around relationships, the hardships and the healing and then guided them through a creative process of writing their own poems. At the end of the workshop series, I was gifted with the task of writing a collective love poem that wove the students works together and shared the heartbeat of their experience. The next phase of the project had me collaborating with a music composer to put the poetry to music. In the end, the output was a multimedia ninety second music video as well as installation of the students' works on campus. My creative heart was fulfilled, inspired and empowered. And I knew that this creative work needed to take a far bigger role in my world—professionally and personally.

A seed of my future had been planted. And my old life in Singapore was disintegrating rapidly.

Out the other side of grief and goodbyes was new life. I felt it running through my veins. Impulse. Direction. Desire. Movement. And so, I followed it. I could feel a big pivot was in order. Some kind of shedding or re-ordering. I knew that it needed time and space.

I spent many mornings grieving my old life. Walking up and down the sand at the beach, only a short walk away from my new Sydney home. And writing. Poetry was flowing out of me.

Within just a few months, I had written fifty love poems. They were so raw, deep and an important part of my personal process. But it also felt like they were the bones of a new book... about love. Heartbreak. Loss. Power. The pain and the beauty of it.

As I welcomed my inner mermaid poet to lead my process, I also welcomed the support of the village. Joseph and his partner. My father. My sister and her family. The Sydney school mums who had welcomed my children into the fold so warmly.

But although the kids were settling in well, I had no idea who I was anymore or where I belonged. Existential exile. Sydney was full of ghosts of the past. And Singapore no longer felt like home. It had been somewhat cutting how quickly many of my connections fell away when I left. I felt like a turtle without a shell. A mermaid who couldn't find her underwater city, with no handsome prince to carry her to a pretty castle in sight. Lost.

The one thing I did know was that this book was coming. And so was winter. I was dreading the cold. I decided to take a risk. I welcomed the blessings of my homeland and my kin, knowing that my children were safe and secure, and hopped on a plane to Greece for the summer. Sydney would wait.

Single. Supported. Ready to write. Ready to create the next version of myself… whoever she was. And surely, just surely, there would be a Greek god (or two) in my future.

As we welcome grief, we welcome love. As we let go of all that is not love, we evolve into a version of ourselves who is ready to give and receive the kind of love that we have been craving all along.

No Other Lovers
Volume #2

The next book in the *Love Sex Poetry Peace* series is coming soon!

What will a summer in Greece bring Lena? Will there be a Greek god involved like she hopes for? What will life be like when she returns to settle into Sydney?

Lena explores a whole new chapter, dips into the Sydney dating pool, encounters some past lovers and finally enters a committed relationship. Who is the lucky guy? Have we met him already... or is he a new beau?

In this volume, Lena will have to work through all her fears of letting love in again... a world with no other lovers... just one love .

Register to receive updates on pre-order information for No Other Lovers

www.nataliarachel.com

NO OTHER LOVERS

Natalia Rachel

Sneak Peak!

Shut Up Spirit Boy

Shapeshifting

Telling me exactly

What I wanted to hear

So I would soften

Into your arms

And drench myself

In the lusty fantasy

That you'd never

Play out.

I would tingle and melt

When you held the door open

And spoke of the

Dreamy future

That my little girl was

Programmed

To believe in and yearn for.

Subtle signs of neglect

And big bad world

Brainwashing.

Every time I began

To bring down

My defenses

And yield into

The potential picture

You were painting

You'd pull back

Push back

Disappear

For a while.

Or you'd tell me

It was too much

Too fast

You need space

You're not ready

The mantra of the

Avoidant male.

I'd never know

If I was meant to

Plead

Play it cool

Or pull back

What's a love-starved

Girl to do?

No matter which

Path I chose

And darling

Trust me

I've walked them all a

Thousand fucking times

It would end in you

Shapeshifting

Again.

Turning up

With some story

Telling me I was

A good girl

Or a bad girl

Scrambling my psyche

So I had no idea

How to behave

Anymore.

Every time

You told me

You valued

My fierce

Protective parts

You were

Appeasing

Your own monster

Telling yourself

It was ok

To treat me

With less care

Than I deserved.

Enabling your

Reckless mouth

And disheveled cock

To say and do whatever

They felt like

In any moment.

The lips of a saint

The tongue of the devil

The arms of an angel

The thrust of some

Playboy.

Zero accountability.

Three-year-old

Boundaries

Fifteen-year-old

Urgency

And the body of a

Grown-ass man

Lashing about

With all the conscious

Bells and whistles

That girls go mad for.

Your conscious tongue

Laced with the shadows

Of your bonded brothers

Is the most dangerous drug

On the dating market.

Shut up, spirit boy

Put your pants on

And go to therapy.

A heart in process is always unavailable. No matter how much love it oozes. No matter how shiny the avatar it beats inside. And a shiny oozy healing heart was my greatest weakness. Especially when it was Dexter's.

Two weeks before I was set to fly out for two months in Greece, my phone lit up with Dexter's call. For a moment, I froze. We hadn't spoken in six weeks. He'd faded into the library of lover's past. But, if I'm honest, I'd kept a loving bookmark in our story, hoping that we were taking a pause between chapters, rather than ending the story altogether. I took a regulating breath and answered. "Dexter... hey."

"Chica! I'm coming to Australia!"

"What for?" I blurted.

My naïve heart whispered, *Could it be for me?*

"I'm going to be co-facilitating this men's retreat. The teacher ran some stuff here at my place in Austin, and when he told me he was going to run some stuff in Sydney, I was like, hell yeah. I'm go going to go breathe with some Aussies, surf and see Lena while I'm at it."

I was an afterthought. That was the first thing that went through my mind. But it was quickly covered with excitement. Dexter was coming to Sydney. And he wanted to see me. I wasn't going to say no to that. I was going to keep my mind and heart open and my feet firmly on the ground.

He was coming for five days only. He landed on a Thursday morning and had two days before supporting a weekend retreat and then Monday to recover before flying out early Tuesday morning. I was due to leave the following day, Wednesday, for two months in Greece. In some ways it was perfect. I'd see him Thursday/Friday, be with my kids on the weekend, and then maybe see him Monday. We decided to play that by ear.

"I can't wait to see you, Chica. I've been going deep into my healing since we last connected. I've been going to men's groups twice a week and done two mushroom journeys. And I can feel my heart opening, and I can feel my masculine energy centering and growing. I can't wait to see if you feel a difference in my energy."

"Sounds really great. Happy you're feeling a shift," I validated. The same part of me that noticed I was an afterthought noticed that he was really focusing on himself and hadn't even asked me how I was. The same part of me that brushed it aside and focused on the excitement that he wanted to see me did exactly the same thing—validated his self-focus. Of course he was talking about himself. He was excited and wanted to share with me. There'd be plenty of time to catch up properly when he arrived.

I'd offered to have him stay at my place for the first two nights before he joined the men at the retreat venue on Saturday morning. And as is my loving way, I decided to go all out to make him feel welcome when he arrived. Fresh sheets and fresh towels. Fresh fruit and croissants. Coffee. Bone broth brewing for later (it was my secret jetlag cure) and some liquid magnesium to help him sleep that evening.

My apartment smelt like basil, mandarins and jasmine and the faint scent of incense. I'd been burning candles and smudging with sage to clear the energy for Dexter's arrival. I was nervous. I kept putting lip gloss on. Checking my appearance in the mirror. I was wearing a pale green cotton bodysuit with a low lace v neck, tiny denim shorts, and a bright pink silk kimono. My sexy goddess at home look. I felt somewhat confused. We had ended things. I was moving on. I told him I didn't want him with such careless loveless parameters. Yet, he was about to walk into my new apartment to stay for two nights, and all I could think of was slipping off my shorts and climbing into bed with him. My clitoris was calling "Dexter, Dexter, Dexter. Come find me, cowboy."

I was lost in the lusty vision of it all when the buzzer rang. He was here! I strode over to the intercom and buzzed it and said in my most nonchalant voice, "Come up."

I opened the front door and draped myself across the frame as I listened to him carry his case up the two flights of stairs to my apartment. My building was a walk up, no elevator. I saw the top of his head, and then his face with his giant smile beaming at me as he approached the top.

"Chica!" he exclaimed.

"Dex," I replied.

He put his bag down and walked up close to me, gazing into my eyes. I didn't move. I even held my breath. He scooped his hands around my waist and pulled me in for a hug. I melted into him, nuzzling into his neck. He kissed my hair. "I missed you, Lena. I really did."

He pulled back to look me in the eye again. I could feel my emotions rising and didn't know how to respond.

"Come in. Welcome to Sydney."

He came in and surveyed the sun-drenched living space.

"This place is magic," he said.

Since repatriating from Singapore to Sydney, I'd moved into a small apartment close to the beach. I'd spent a lot of time making it feel wonderful. Full of whites, turquoise and natural tones. A real high-end beach pad feeling. I loved my new place, and it felt nice to have him compliment it.

"Coffee?" I gestured for him to sit on the sofa and poured us both some French press.

"I feel like I'm in a dream," he said. "I just can't stop smiling. I can't believe I am here with you."

"I'm happy you're here," I said.

We sat and sipped coffee, and Dexter told me all about the men's retreat he was facilitating and shared some deep insights that he'd uncovered during his recent mushroom journeys.

"I realize I never felt love from my dad. And that made me feel like a burden. Or like I had to be better to get his approval. And then that felt like a burden. And I just started looking for burdens. My wife became a burden. My business became a burden. And you know what, I think I turned you into a burden too."

My stomach clenched. What was he trying to say?

"You're not, by the way. And I know you tried to tell me that, but I couldn't hear you. I just wasn't ready to hear you. You're a gift. The real deal."

My stomach clenched a little more. And I pursed my lips. But at the same time, I felt wildly turned on.

"I don't know what to say, Dex... I'm glad you're doing the work."

"Yeah, it's been incredible," he continued. "I'm seeing the world in a whole new way."

After coffee, I asked if he'd like a shower after the long flight. He took the invitation and disappeared into the bathroom for a while. I could hear him singing in the shower. Some folky love song. His voice sent shivers of lust through me. Even my toes and eyelashes felt turned on. I lay on the sofa, feeling my own desire and trying to regulate myself a little. He came out of the bathroom, still slightly damp, with my favorite dark green towel wrapped around his waist.

"Let's take a nap. I want to hold you, Chica."

I got up silently and walked towards him with a smile, took his hand, and led him into my bedroom. I slid my shorts off and let my kimono fall to the floor and sprawled out on my bed. "You're ready to nap?" I asked, amused.

He let his towel drop to the ground with a big grin and climbed on top of me. "Not quite yet," he said as he stroked my hair and leaned forward to take in my scent. "I remember your smell. You smell so good to me. Like the universe or something."

We spent the next four hours making love slowly. Whispering to each other. Dozing. And as I was basking in the oxytocin ocean of it all, he whispered in my ear, "This could be a beautiful life here, Chica. Together. Couldn't it? I can see it. I can feel it."

It was like every fantasy about having a conscious boyfriend I'd ever had was birthing in that moment. "It could be beautiful," I replied. 'It is beautiful. Right now."

We spent the next two days exploring my neighborhood. Drinking flat whites, walking the beach, eating fish and chips and hopping into bed between activities. There'd be these moments where he would pause and tell me how he can see the vision. Us. A potential timeline. He'd do it a few times a day. And I could feel myself getting lost in the dream with him. Forgetting that he'd told me less than two months prior that he didn't want a relationship. Forgetting that he'd told me he wanted to fuck around. Forgetting that he had four young kids, an ex-wife, papers to sign, a giant mortgage and no stable income. Lost in his words. Lost in my own chemical rush. The bubble that was always destined to pop.

On the morning that he was going to leave for the men's retreat, we woke, had melty morning sex, and I cooked him a healthy breakfast. Leek and parmesan omelet with a side of kale, and a slice of sourdough with hummus. After finishing he said, "This has been amazing. I feel loved. Taken care of. I feel like a fucking man when I'm with you. A capable man." He leaned over and stroked my hair. "I'm going to go silent for the next two days, m'kay? Really focus on holding space for these other men. And I feel so full and ready to do that. And I guess I'll talk to you out the other side, ok?"

I was lost for words. Confused. Again. It was like I was reliving the time he told me he needed a week of silence and anticipated the excruciating pain of it all. But I reminded myself this was different. He was entering sacred space. Of course he wanted to honor it. And it was two days. I'd see him again on Monday. For sure.

"Of course, Dex, I'll look forward to reconnecting out the other side."

He gave me a deep goodbye kiss and said, "You're a life changing kinda woman, Lena. See ya."

I spent the next two days on an oxytocin high. My kids came for the weekend, and we went on beach walks, kicked the ball, cooked dinner together and played their favorite card games. And while I was present and in it with them, a small part of my psyche was occupied, replaying some of the sweet moments with Dexter, or imagining what our future in Sydney could look like.

Joseph came to collect the kids around five pm on Sunday. Exactly the time that Dexter's retreat was finishing. After I kissed the kids goodbye, my anxiety started to kick in. Dexter and I hadn't planned to speak, but I expected he would call. Hoping that he couldn't wait till Monday to see me and would rush over and take me in his arms. As I sat with my hope and my worry, I realized we hadn't made a plan at all. So, I decided to text him.

How was the retreat? Can't wait to hear about it. What are you up to?

Immediately after I sent the text, my anxiety skyrocketed. What if he thought that was insecure, or grabby or that I wasn't honoring his space or his agency? I decided to do some stretching, have a bath and cook dinner and just focus on myself. By eight thirty pm, I still hadn't heard anything. I felt sad. A little annoyed. A little worried. He's probably integrating. Or out with the men to celebrate. Or sleeping.

I was coaching myself into a false calm. Into excusing his silence.

I slept fitfully that night. Waking every two or three hours and checking my phone. Monday passed. And I heard nothing. What the fuck? This felt rude. Mean. Hurtful. I'd cleared my schedule and evening to spend the day and night with him before he flew out. And there I was, sitting waiting for a man that clearly was not coming. How did I get back here again? I was so frustrated with myself. But there was also that part of me that was self-pathologizing, making excuses for him and hoping he would reach out with some understandable story that would make it all better.

After another fitful night of waiting, hoping, worrying and soothing myself, still nothing. I knew he was due to flight out Tuesday morning. I was in the middle of meditating on my balcony. Strangely, I could feel Dexter's energy. I looked up. Was he here? On his way to me? His flight was due out in two hours. He should be at the airport by now. I picked up my phone. And there it was. A five minute voice note.

Chica, I hope you're good. Sorry I didn't make it back to your place to see ya before flying out.... The men's retreat was wild... so much healing.... Ended up taking some mushrooms on Sunday night with a women's retreat group that had been running at the same center... six men and six women all doing deep healing work... I connected with this one woman.... I think she is my soul mate... nomadic yoga teacher... my heart fully opened.... She's coming to Austin with me... going to hang for a while... nothing serious... just following the energy of it... don't really know what I am doing... but I think we shouldn't talk anymore... not forever... but just for now... I think I need to protect you by giving you space.... Giving myself space... you really are amazing... I love everything about you.... But yeah, this is me signing out... I don't know how long for... not forever... for now.... Love you, Chica. Bye.

As I listened to the message, I could finally see exactly who he was. A wounded little boy.

An image of Lucas fucking those two women flashed through my mind, and I winced, reliving the pain of the past. In some ways, this felt similar. But with Lucas, the toxicity had been on display. Overt. He was aware of his own darkness. Whereas Dexter had totally dissociated from the truth of who he was. His spiritual persona made him far more dangerous. A dangerous dickhead. Completely unconscious. Explaining away his horrific behavior. Gaslighting me. Gaslighting his own consciousness. So much shadow.

And as I saw, I was done. No anger. No grief. Just relief that the spell had been broken for good. I did not warrant his voice note with a reply. Instead, I took a shower and cleansed myself of his energy. Changed my sheets. Saged the house. Packed for my flight to Greece. And walked out into the sunshine of my life.

Stay Tuned...

www.nataliarachel.com

Heal for Love Multi-media Series

If you've loved following Lena's journey to heal for love, now's the chance to do your own healing work.

The Heal for Love multi-media series is a bridge between fantasy and reality. Tune into a series of 'commentaries on love' where I unpack what it means to love and be loved in our modern world... and why so many of us are finding the love we have dreamed of illusive. Explore author readings, poetry performances and delve into self-inquiry exercises that will have you Re-imaging your own love life... just like Lena.

About Natalia Rachel

Natalia Rachel writes to touch the heart, open the mind and inspire new ways of living, relating and weaving our world.

Her latest work *Love Sex Poetry Peace* is a genre bending, women's fiction trilogy that shares a modern female perspective on relationships, romance, healing, parenthood and community. Instead of traditional romance tropes, Natalia explores the realities of dating and partnership amidst a middle-aged app-driven dating pool for women who are saying no to traditional relationship narratives and focussing on their self-development and fulfilment. She hopes that the protagonist, Lena, and her four female friends serve as modern role models to women who are navigating their own love lives. The work includes in her very personal poetry which she wrote while processing her own love life. She's taken great pleasure in creating a tapestry of fantasy, reality, poetry and narrative driven stories. The work was inspired by not only her own journey, but the stories of her close friends and some of her therapy clients who are also learning to love later in life.

Before Natalia decided to explore the world of fiction, she released her first non-fiction book *Why am I like this? Illuminating the traumatized self*, that came out with Penguin Random House in 2022. The book blends philosophy, memoir, self-inquiry questions and somatic exercises for the reader to go on their own journey to heal from trauma and live a more connected life.

Natalia is also the creative lead behind *The Living Poetry Project*, a process-oriented multi-media production that inspires Australian youths to explore their own relationship narratives through poetry.

From the age of seven, Natalia has used the power of poetry and prose to help herself and others make sense of complex, often unarticulated experiences, that release shame, inspire hope, and call us all to radical accountability and deeper compassion. Her words are both profound, playful and make it safe to start exploring the unseen and unexpressed. Her mission is to unearth the things we can't quite put our finger on or are too afraid to say. A selection of her *Poetry Anthology* is available online.

Aside from her work as a writer, Natalia is a therapist and facilitator who has worked with individuals and groups in the United States of America, United Kingdom, Europe, Asia, Australia and New Zealand. The global nature of her work continues to inspire reflections on the struggles of humanity and the path to our shared liberation. She is currently based in Sydney, Australia where she enjoys mornings at the beach, time with her two children and keeping a quiet rhythm between projects.

www.nataliarachel.com

natalia@illumahealth.org

@lspp_theseries
@natalia_rachel_change

www.nataliarachel.com

Natalia Rachel